Destination:
Monterey

Destination: Monterey
A Destination Murder Mystery

Ann Shepphird

4 Horsemen
Publications, Inc.

Destination: Monterey
Destination Murder Mysteries Book 2
Copyright © 2022 Ann Shepphird. All rights reserved.

4 Horsemen
Publications, Inc.

4 Horsemen Publications, Inc.
1497 Main St. Suite 169
Dunedin, FL 34698
4horsemenpublications.com
info@4horsemenpublications.com

Typesetting by Michelle Cline
Editor Jen Paquette

All rights to the work within are reserved to the author and publisher. No part of this publication may be reproduced, stored in a retrieval system, or transmitted in any form or by any means, electronic, mechanical, photocopying, recording, scanning, or otherwise, except as permitted under Section 107 or 108 of the 1976 International Copyright Act, without prior written permission except in brief quotations embodied in critical articles and reviews. Please contact either the Publisher or Author to gain permission.

This book is meant as a reference guide. All characters, organizations, and events portrayed in this novel are either products of the author's imagination or are used fictitiously. All brands, quotes, and cited work respectfully belong to the original rights holders and bear no affiliation to the authors or publisher.

Library of Congress Control Number: 2022936709

Print ISBN: 978-1-64450-600-4
Audio ISBN: 978-1-64450-599-1
eBook ISBN: 978-1-64450-601-1

For my mom, Jane Woodson

Thank you to all who helped bring this book
to life, especially Amy Akiona, Jill Bastian,
Erika Lance, Kathleen Matschullat,
Jen Paquette, Jon Reynolds, Jordan Weiner,
Valerie Willis, and Jeff Wolf.

CHAPTER ONE

I balked. I'll admit it. Totally balked. I didn't think it was a good idea. I mean, here I was, fresh off my first press trip as a travel writer—to a luxury resort on Maui, no less—and instead of flying off to a new exotic locale, I was being asked to write a story about Monterey County. I mean, sure, the area surrounding my hometown of Carmel-by-the-Sea, California, has incredible scenery and attractions—not to mention a variety of world-class hotels—from Big Sur to Pebble Beach that other people would kill to write about (ha—not literally!). I still had two pretty substantial reasons why covering it didn't sit well with me.

The first was that after a taste of the thrill that comes with getting on a plane and heading thousands of miles away to a new adventure, it felt a little pedestrian to be knocking around the place where I grew up. The second, and if I'm honest—more compelling, reason was that I had only recently left my old life as an investigative reporter in Los Angeles and returned to Carmel to help take care of my ailing father, taking a part-time job as the travel columnist for *Carmel Today* magazine in the process. While so far it wasn't too bad being back and I enjoyed my new job, let's just say I had my reasons for staying away from Carmel-by-the-Sea—cute little hamlet that it is—for the dozen-or-so years after I left for college.

So, yeah, I'll admit I balked a little when I was first given the assignment. I will say, though, that once all was said and done, I not only gained a new appreciation for the area as one of the most special places on earth; I also managed to save a life and solve a mysterious disappearance along the way.

Of course, that's all well and good in retrospect. It just didn't feel that way at first. Part of it was the way it was presented to me by my editor-in-chief at *Carmel Today* magazine, Mona Reynolds.

"Not every assignment is to a luxury resort in a tropical paradise, Sam," Mona said, in a rather sarcastic tone that I am going to admit did not sit well with me. Not at all. It didn't help that the rest of the staff sitting in the magazine's conference room started chuckling. Even her damn dog Cornwall—a tiny yorkie-poo she'd adopted as part of Carmel's unwritten edict that everyone have a pooch at their side—seemed to smirk.

Et tu, Cornwall? *Et tu*?

Chapter One

Mona was not only the editor-in-chief at *Carmel Today* magazine, but she was also the longtime family friend who had offered me the travel-writer gig when I returned to town. Now in her early 60s, Mona was tall and lean, and always impeccably dressed. In short, Mona still looked like she stepped right out of the pages of *Vogue* magazine, where she had been a long-time features editor. Like me, Mona had grown up in Carmel and had only returned to town herself the previous year when she was offered the editor-in-chief position.

The chuckles and smirks from my colleagues really weren't warranted, in my opinion. I mean, all I had done was mention that focusing our "Splendid Adventures" column—the longer travel feature I was responsible for each month—on our backyard (as it were) wasn't the most exciting thing in the world. Especially coming on the heels of what ended up being a scintillating (if I do say so myself) piece on the luxurious Mokihana Resort & Spa on the Hawaiian island of Maui.

Okay, so that had been my first real travel feature and my first press trip. It had also included the drama (if you want to call it that) of the murder of one of my fellow travel writers and a burgeoning romance with the detective on the case, Roger Kai, with whom I may or may not have exchanged more than a few texts, phone calls, and video chats since my return (I may). As I fiddled with the braided leather bracelet he gave me before I left Maui, I thought about our last lingering hug and kiss, and the way his hand brushed mine just before we said goodbye.

As you can see, the bar was set pretty high for my next "Splendid Adventures" story. My argument was that the smaller "Out and About" pieces I wrote for the front newsy section of the magazine were specifically designed to cover the greater Monterey region, so it would be a bit redundant to then cover similar content in the bigger travel feature. And, okay, I was looking forward to whatever exotic locale I might be sent to next.

But no. Mona was instead proposing that I create a travel story out of the hidden gems people could visit in and around the Monterey Peninsula, which was not only where *Carmel Today* was based (obviously), but where I had grown up. Exotic, at least for me, it was not. As Mona explained, the timing of the issue we were discussing—which would come out the same month as the annual Pebble Beach Pro-Am golf tournament—was perfect for a feature highlighting the tourism delights to be found in Monterey County locales from Pacific Grove to Big Sur.

Because the issue would easily be the biggest of the year and thus attract more eyeballs (and advertisers), this meant more pages for editorial and a group effort to really shine. That was the speech Mona was giving to the troops, anyway. It was going to be her first Pebble Beach Pro-Am issue since taking over the magazine, and she

Chapter One

really wanted to impress the new owners with what *Carmel Today* was capable of after its years of neglect under the previous editor. Again (and I realize I'm pressing the issue here), this is why I had to question the fact she wanted my "Splendid Adventures" story to focus on local sites.

"Our readers, especially for this issue, include a fair share of tourists," said Mona, running her fingers through her gorgeous shock of silver hair before straightening her designer glasses, which somehow matched a patch of red in the silk scarf she wore.

"And we have a number of local advertisers that want to reach those tourists," added Stacy Peterson, the magazine's associate publisher, with a gleaming smile that matched the color of her platinum blonde hairstyle. It was Stacy's job to oversee the sales staff — two young gals named Nina and Simone (I kid you not) who dressed just like her — so I wasn't sure how I felt about her weighing in on the destinations we covered. To me, that should be a strictly editorial function. But as I had learned since starting my job at the magazine, things were very different than they were back at my former job on the Metro team at the newspaper, where I never even knew who the advertising people were. At a small magazine like this one, the "separation of church and state" as they called the differentiation between editorial and advertising was a bit more porous.

I listened as Stiletto Stacy — my nickname for her (in my mind only, of course, and something

I had started as a way to remember people's names)—continued to make her pitch. Stacy talked about how the advertisers would like the region covered as a way to entice readers to hang around and explore (and spend a little more money in the process) in the days before and/or after the golf tournament. As she spoke, I plastered on my best corporate smile. It helped me to not do what I really wanted to do—say, inadvertently drop a copy of the magazine down on her always impeccable (if not particularly practical) nails, whose color often—but not always—matched the stilettos.

Instead, I looked over at Tom Morgan, the longtime (and from what I could see long-suffering) managing editor of the magazine sitting next to Stacy, to see if he might back me up. Tom was one of the older staff members who, as Mona liked to put it, "came with the magazine" when she took it over. Unlike some of the others, though, Tom was one she was more than happy to retain. He was both very competent and a link to the Carmel scene that she had been away from for more than 30 years. A bit curmudgeonly (don't tell him but I mentally called him Toupee Tom, because, well, it was ridiculously obvious just what it was sitting on top of his dome there), Tom was typical of the type I had dealt with growing up with a dad who worked in law enforcement and in my years at the newspaper. Truthfully, I prided myself on my ability to deal with curmudgeons and so far

Chapter One

had only garnered praise from him for the copy I turned in, which was both clean and on deadline.

Sitting next to Tom was Ben Conners, the production designer. Ben was a newer addition to the staff and a necessary one, with all the new graphics and video additions to the magazine's digital edition that Mona was making. With long hair, a few tattoos, and wearing the young geek uniform of jeans and comic book-inspired t-shirts, Ben would fit in easily with the crowd at Comic-Con, where I once covered a story for the newspaper about an altercation between a few Klingons that turned violent. Thus, his moniker was (again, in my mind only) "Ben Comic-Conners." Decent guy, from what I had gleaned so far, but happier with his nose in his computer than anywhere else.

As my gaze continued to make its way around the room, Mona took Stacy's place in discussing their idea for a destination story highlighting the area surrounding our base in Carmel-by-the-Sea.

"Don't worry. We're not asking you to visit every inch of Monterey County—only a few select places that have news or some specific historic significance to highlight," said Mona. "The idea is to capture the heart of the Monterey area. Everybody knows about the golf, obviously, but the region is so much more than that and, as our travel writer, I would love for you to capture it."

Okay. That was fair and a little intriguing and maybe it wouldn't be too bad. But then Mona continued… "To help you out—and because we are getting a little close to starting production on the issue in order to get it out in time for the event—while you were in Maui, I asked Chelsea to start creating a little itinerary for you, with input from the rest of us on the staff and the folks at the various local tourism bureaus, of course."

Mona smiled and looked over at the youngest member of the team: Chelsea Plumrose. Ugh. Chelsea started at *Carmel Today* only a few months before I did, and as a recent college graduate was maybe a decade younger. Like Stacy, she had blond hair, but instead of fluffed platinum, hers was long and highlight-streaked and pulled back into a perky ponytail. In addition to the ubiquitous ponytail, her tiny frame was almost always outfitted in black knee-high boots, tight pants or leggings, and a short blazer. This, she constantly informed us, was part of her "professional personal branding." If that wasn't annoying enough, in her few months at the magazine, Chelsea had already managed to piss off just about everybody on the staff with her haughty attitude and snarky comments.

When I agreed to take the job, Mona had confided in me that Chelsea was a bit of a political hire, but Mona seemed to have a lot more faith that her (shall we say) youthful exuberance just needed a little fine tuning than I did. The niece of the new owners, Chelsea had just completed journalism school—something that was apparent within the first five minutes of talking to her as she parroted seemingly everything she learned

Chapter One

from her professors (some of whom were ones who gave instructors the "those who can't do, teach" stereotype) at every possible turn. Having started just before I came on board, she was not particularly happy with my arrival as she would have enjoyed taking over the travel-related columns—something she let me know within minutes of meeting me. She also let me know, in no uncertain terms, where I fell in the hierarchy: I was just a part-time columnist; Chelsea was the full-time editorial coordinator.

By this point, you are probably wondering, so I will come out and tell you that my internal nickname for her was Fuck You Chelsea (aka FU Chelsea).

"Thank you, Mona," said Chelsea, beaming her perkiest beam. (Is a perky beam a thing? If so, she'd perfected it). "Sam, as you will see on the list of places I've put together for you to visit over the next week or so, we're looking to do something similar to those '36 hours' pieces that run in the *New York Times*. You are all familiar with the *New York Times*, correct?"

Chelsea took a moment to look around the table and, well, let's just say that if lasers were attached to the incredulous looks Chelsea was getting, she would be burned to a crisp on the spot. Yes, FU Chelsea, we've heard of the *New York Times*.

"We would like to do something like that about all the amazing things you can do in and around the Monterey Peninsula the days before and after the Pebble Beach Pro-Am. Kind of a 'road to Pebble Beach.' Get it?" Chelsea squealed with joy at her own cleverness before continuing. "Thus, we'll start with things like the wineries and golf resorts in Carmel Valley, then head down to highlight a new art exhibit and restaurant in Big Sur before swinging back up through the towns of Monterey and Pacific Grove and ending up in Pebble Beach itself, which as you all may know is where the golf tournament takes place…"

More lasers from the staffers, most of whom (like me) had lived and/or worked on the Monterey Peninsula their whole lives and were quite aware of where the PEBBLE BEACH Pro-Am takes place.

"We will, of course, also include the quaint shops, eateries, and galleries of Carmel-by-the-Sea itself." Oh, she was proud of herself, Chelsea was. "To that end, I have created this for you, Sam."

Chelsea handed me a glossy folder that I opened to find an itinerary similar to the one the public relations firm had put together for my Maui trip. It even included a header: "Road to Pebble Beach Monterey County Itinerary for Samantha Powers." Based on a first glance, Chelsea had taken the time to create the itinerary in InDesign (versus, you know, a Word document like any normal person might) and inserted pictures illustrating each place. Yes, pictures.

"You'll note in the itinerary that I have created in consultation with, among others, my

Chapter One

new friend Katie over at the Monterey tourism bureau…" said Chelsea. And then, as if reading the room a bit: "I also consulted with Mona and Stacy, of course."

"Of course."

"I've done my best to lump the areas and items of interest together to make it easier for you to tell the story of the 'Road to Pebble Beach.' As you know, we had already identified this week's opening of the music venue at the Carmel Valley winery and the new show at the Perch Gallery in Big Sur as things we wanted to cover in the 'Out and About' section, so we worked the beginning of your itinerary around those." More glee-filled eyes to celebrate her own creativity.

"We have you starting in Carmel Valley in one of the recently renovated rooms at the Carmel Valley Golf Lodge. You can check out the rooms and the resort itself before and after you cover the opening of the music venue. It's actually a perfect place to start the piece because, well, as we all know part of the theme is GOLF!"

The glee with which she said that was so over the top that I had a hard time squelching a laugh.

"After that, you will head down to Big Sur, where the owners who renovated the Wildflower Inn recently brought on a new chef and reopened their restaurant. They were nice enough to invite you to stay at the inn and check out the restaurant before you hit the artist reception at Perch. After that, you will come back through Carmel-by-the-Sea, where you might spend some time over the weekend to see what's new downtown," Chelsea said, looking at me and pointing to the itinerary. "I highlighted some suggestions."

Gee, thanks, I thought as I flipped through the packet.

"Then you will head out to Monterey, where Katie can show you the new exhibit at the aquarium. I should mention you might meet up with some golf writers the bureau invited to tour the town before the pro-am press preview while you are there. Finally, you will swing through Pacific Grove to see the updates that have been made to the historic Asilomar property before ending up in Pebble Beach to check out the site of the tournament itself."

As Chelsea continued to natter along, everyone seemed to have gone into some kind of coma as indicated by their glazed-over eyes. I couldn't tell how Mona was feeling about Chelsea's taking over the meeting. To me, it was totally disrespectful to Mona, and let's be honest here, *me*. I kept looking over to see if Mona was going to step up and quash Chelsea with a correction. But, no, Mona braved a stiff smile as she let Chelsea continue on before delivering the kicker.

"…and, Sam, I have been thinking that it might be best for you to pass this story by me before turning it in to Tom and Mona," said Chelsea. "You know, to correct any bad habits you've fallen into."

I'm sorry, what the…? Who does this little recent J-school punk think she is? I had a good ten years of

Chapter One

experience on her. Plus, if I was being honest, one of the perks of this job had been my easy access to Mona—something she promised me wouldn't change. I looked over to see Mona's reaction to Chelsea's statement, but she turned away to give Cornwall a little pet as if she couldn't stand to even meet my gaze. I turned back to Chelsea's smug smile. That smug sanctimonious smile. Sigh. I mean, I knew she was the niece of the owners, but what could she possibly have on Mona for her to let her be so egregiously disrespectful?

"Sam doesn't have any bad habits that I've seen, Chelsea." It wasn't Mona but Tom who stood up for me, the scalp under his toupee getting increasingly red. "As I am still the managing editor—as far as I know," he said, looking pointedly at Mona, "all copy will continue to go through me."

That certainly got everybody's attention. Every head at the table slowly turned to look back at Mona.

"Of course, you are, Tom," Mona said, turning to look back at Chelsea. "Chelsea, you will continue to proof the stories in the magazine once it has all been laid out, but Tom is still the one they go through first."

Now it was Chelsea's turn to get a little red. Oh, aren't staff meetings fun.

"Well, I for one can't wait to work my column around the golf tournament," Terry Cummings, one of the magazine's oldest of old-timers (and "Tottering Terry" to me), said, breaking the tension.

Not really on staff, but still invited to the editorial planning meetings, Terry wrote one of those "how I see things" types of columns on a freelance basis each month. Although it verged on parody, Mona couldn't outright kill the column—Terry was an old friend of both the old owner and the new owners, and part of the old-timer Carmel clique Mona needed to make sure not to alienate. She did consign the column to the real estate ads that ran in the back of the magazine.

"I can talk about the hijinks that went on during the early days of the Crosby Clambake," said Terry. "That's what they originally called the golf tournament, you know, in honor of Bing Crosby, who created the event. When I was just a kid and would work as a volunteer, all the players would get drunk and ride around in their carts ogling the pretty girls. One year, one of them filled gallon jugs with martinis…"

"Thank you, Terry," Mona said, with an almost imperceptible sigh as she stroked Cornwall's back a little more manically.

"Then there was the year it snowed and the boys…"

"Thank you, Terry," Mona said a little more forcefully. "I'm sure you will do a wonderful job with your column."

"That one's going to need a ton of editing," Chelsea mumbled under her breath, getting a withering look from both Terry and Tom in response.

Chapter One

"Now, Sam, when you look at the itinerary that we *all*," Mona said, pointedly looking at everyone, "put together, you'll notice it includes two events that the magazine will also be involved with on the marketing side as part of the issue's promotion. Stacy, of course, will be spearheading those. Stacy?"

"Of course, Mona," said Stacy. "As you all know, the owners of *Carmel Today*—Bob and Barb Carpenter—are opening a new music venue at their winery's tasting room out in Carmel Valley. In addition to you covering the event, Sam, we will be using it to help market the issue. A number of us on the sales side will be attending, as will potential advertisers and golf industry insiders in town for next week's Pebble Beach press event, which we have agreed to sponsor part of as well. As Chelsea noted, we worked your trip around those two events and then added in the other elements of interest and did it all in consultation with the local tourism bureaus and the hotel public relations teams."

Okay, okay, I get it—you all created it together, I thought. *Can we move on now?*

Stacy turned to me in a way that blocked out my view of FU Chelsea and seemed to be trying to assure me with her eyes. "I think you will see it really is a well-rounded look at the area. You might even find some things that surprise you, Sam."

If Stacy only knew how true those words would turn out to be.

CHAPTER TWO

With the rest of the editorial line-up set and the stories all assigned for the special Pebble Beach Pro-Am issue, most of the staff got back to the task of getting the current issue off to the printer. My work on that issue was already done—and as Chelsea often informed me, I was only supposed to be in the office part-time and had to keep my hours under a certain number each month—so I packed up my things and prepared to head out for the day.

As I walked through the office, I could see FU Chelsea standing over Ben at his computer in the art department. Ben had the hunchbacked look of the oppressed as Chelsea pointed to something on his screen.

Chapter Two

"See how the type is touching where the em-dash meets the 't'? You can just add a little kerning to get rid of that..."

"It's like Buddy never left," said Tom, looking at the two of them and shaking his head as I passed.

"Buddy?" I asked.

"The former editor-in-chief of *Carmel Today*. Buddy Wheeler. He had a thing about touching type."

"Boy, did he," Stiletto Stacy piped up as she joined us looking over at the unfolding scene. "Even with the marketing materials, we would spend hours adding imperceptible little spaces between the 'r' and the 'm' in the *Carmel Today* logo."

"Why?" I asked.

"Heaven forbid the type touches," said Tom.

"Not just touches, even appears to be close to touching," said Stacy.

"Does anybody really notice that?" I asked.

"Buddy did," both Tom and Stacy said at the same time.

"Now, if he wrote an editorial calling the mayor an asshole or, say, insisted we run a story touting a business he'd recently purchased a stake in, those kinds of lines he didn't have trouble crossing," Stacy said.

Tom laughed and then said with a shrug, "I suppose the content was his prerogative as editor-in-chief, even if much of it broke every journalistic edict."

"We will always have those glorious few months last year when you were in charge, Tom," said Stacy, patting his shoulder. "Or even the first few months after Mona came on board."

As Stacy walked off, Tom smiled and then sighed, nodding to Chelsea. "And then this one arrived…"

"Speaking of which, I wanted to say thank you for sticking up for me back there, Tom," I said.

"No problem, Sam. I've always got your back. You're an incredible asset to the magazine."

"Thank you. I appreciate that."

We were interrupted by Chelsea's voice wafting back out. "Then there's a widow on page seven."

"That's not a widow," Tom said loudly so they could hear him. "Stop pestering him, Chelsea. The copy looks fine."

"It's a widow, Tom."

"A widow is when there is only one word left at the bottom of the paragraph. There are two words there. It's fine."

"But they're small words and this just leaves way too much white space on the page."

As Tom's face again started turning red, I gave a quick wave, slipped out the door, and started walking the half dozen blocks over to my friend Lizzy Icaza's dog-friendly cafe, Paws Up. It wasn't the only dog-friendly establishment in Carmel. Not by a long shot. Just the latest in a long tradition. But Lizzy's was the newest and a bit more casual and local-focused, located as

Chapter Two

it was in the courtyard of a building her grandmother owned that was away from the center of town and surrounded by professional offices instead of retail stores.

"Can you believe this garbage?" I said, setting the folder with the itinerary Chelsea had created down on the bar in front of Lizzy.

"I don't see any garbage here," said Lizzy, even though she knew exactly what I meant.

"I'm talking about this," referring to the folder.

"And what exactly is that?"

"An itinerary that FU Chelsea created for me to explore the Monterey Peninsula."

"Fun! That's your new 'Splendid Adventure'?"

"Yup."

"I'm intrigued."

"There's nothing intriguing about it. It's stupid."

"In what way?"

"I'm supposed to be a travel columnist and I'm just exploring the area."

"So … a lot of people travel here," Lizzy said, pointing to a few obvious tourists sitting at the back of her cafe with their pooches at their feet and guidebooks in their hands.

"I'm not saying it shouldn't be written up in other magazines. You know, for people who *travel* here."

"Well, you will be *traveling* to get to Big Sur and Carmel Valley," Lizzy said. "Besides, there's a lot you probably don't know about the area. You have never lived here as an adult, Sam. I can tell you from experience that there are a ton of things I have discovered since I returned home that I never even knew existed as a kid."

"I guess we were kind of single-focused growing up."

"You were focused on getting the hell out of here. Except for your internship at the *Carmel Pine Cone*—and even there they just had you covering the police log because of your dad—your mind was always elsewhere."

"That police log got me in a lot of trouble."

"I forgot about your creative rephrasing of the items. They were pretty funny. I suppose that's the price they paid for putting a teenager in charge. The point is you never did much exploring."

"I guess that's true."

"Nice photos, by the way," Lizzy said, flipping through the itinerary.

"That's the other thing."

"What?"

"It's not Chelsea's place to be assigning me stories or creating itineraries, with or without snazzy photos."

"Sounds like it was Mona's idea and Chelsea was just helping her out."

Sigh. I think you can see that Lizzy was just NOT GETTING IT.

"This actually looks like a lot of fun. What do they call it? A 'staycation'?" Lizzy continued.

"Groan."

"Oh, come on. A lot has changed around here since you left," said Lizzy. "I mean, including college, you've been away for more than a dozen

Chapter Two

years, right? It wouldn't hurt for you to check the area out a little. All you've seen since you returned home is this place, your dad's assisted living facility, and the magazine. That's, what, a three-mile radius?"

"I go to the market." Yes, I knew how stupid I sounded.

She waited as I sulked just a little more before continuing. "You haven't even gotten out on the court with me yet."

"Oh, come on, Lizzy. I haven't played tennis in years and you, well, you have played a LOT."

That was an understatement. Lizzy spent her years away from home traveling the professional tennis tour, where she had achieved some success as a doubles specialist. Lizzy and I actually met as kids on the public tennis courts, but it was pretty evident early on that her skill level far surpassed mine. As sisters in everything but name—Lizzy had six brothers and I was the only child of older parents—our competitiveness was legendary. There was a point where we couldn't even rally on a tennis court without trying to annihilate each other, with most of the annihilating happening to me. That was about the time I started hanging out with the kids on the school newspaper instead of the jocks, but our friendship never wavered.

When Lizzy retired from the tour and came back to town permanently, she was adamant about not taking a job as a tennis pro at one of the many clubs in the area. Instead, she transformed what had been a somewhat decrepit cafe space into the Paws Up. As you may guess, it became my hang-out in the times I wasn't visiting my dad or at the magazine, which were all an easy walk from our family home.

"That doesn't mean we can't get out on a court and just hit," said Lizzy, reaching down to pet her dog Canoodle, a dachshund-schnauzer-lab mix, who in the way of dogs matching their owners looked just like her—long and lean and incredibly athletic, with curly black hair kept short. "It would be fun. And the offer still stands to help me with the kids on the tennis team up at the high school a couple times a week."

"How can I do that when I'll be gallivanting all over Monterey County?" I asked, waving the itinerary around again.

"It doesn't have to be this week and it doesn't have to be all the time, but I think it would help round out your life a little bit to do something other than just work and visit your dad."

"Especially when work sucks."

"Oh, get over yourself, Sam. You're being asked to stay at the nicest hotels in town and visit some pretty cool attractions. Sounds like a great gig to me."

"Yeah, perfect. Except for fucking Chelsea."

"Sam, there are no perfect jobs." As Lizzy said this, a big old Irish wolfhound yakked up something truly heinous in the corner. She looked over at the mess and then back at me. "As I was saying…"

Chapter Two

All right. Point taken. Dealing with Chelsea and cleaning up barf were kind of the same, right?

My next stop on my walk back home from work was my dad's assisted living facility. I waved to the receptionist and the group of ladies who were almost always sitting near the door before heading down the long hall to the memory care center. I pushed the buzzer and looked through the small window. I saw Alejandra, one of my dad's saintly nurse's aides, and waved. She came to open the door and pointed to my dad waiting at his usual pre-dinner spot at the table, looking smaller and more grizzled with each visit.

"How's he doing?" I asked as we walked in his direction.

"Better! We took a group down to the beach today and got him to come along."

"That's great," I said, happy to hear he was joining in the activities they were always planning instead of acting out or hitting people, which had been his usual tendencies.

"It is. He's less anxious and participating more."

"Good to hear. Thank you so much, Alejandra."

I reached the dining room table, sat down across from him, and waited to see if I could find the glint of life behind his eyes that meant he was alert and knew who I was. I was never sure how much I would get. He turned and looked at me, beginning, as always, by looking me up and down and scrutinizing me like I was one of his suspects from back when he was the Carmel police chief.

Then, slowly, as the realization of who he was talking to dawned on him, he asked the dreaded question: "Where's the dog?"

Because of the length of the staff meeting, I hadn't had time to swing by the house to pick up my Uncle Henry's English bulldog. Buster was the latest in a long line of bulldog-related rescue dogs I had grown up with and my usual companion on these visits. It was too bad he wasn't with me as Buster was an unusually good conversation starter and one of the few beings—furry or otherwise—other than me and his brother Henry that my dad still recognized.

"Home with Uncle Henry. I didn't have time to stop and get him today."

"That's too bad."

"Next time."

"Okay."

"How's it going, Dad?"

"Eh."

"Alejandra said you all went down to the beach today."

"Did we?"

"That's what I hear."

"Okay." Then he scrutinized me again and asked me the other question I almost always got. "Following a case?"

Back when I was covering crime at the newspaper in Los Angeles and my dad was still the police chief, our way of communicating had been to share whatever cases we were working on. This was especially true after my mom died.

Chapter Two

She had been the communicator in the family, the one who managed to keep our somewhat contentious relationship under control. After she died, the few times I made it home, my dad and I kept things as superficial as possible—and that meant talking about the one thing we had in common: a love of solving mysteries.

"Not really a case, Dad. Just a new 'Splendid Adventure.'" (Yes, I used air quotes). "This one through the wilds of Monterey County."

He furrowed his brow. "Monterey. That's here."

"You got that right."

"Huh. Who for?"

"*Carmel Today* magazine. Remember, I'm writing about travel now. For Mona. Mona Reynolds."

"Mom's friend."

"Yeah, mom's friend."

"She's back?"

"Yeah, she came back last year. Remember? She visited you on Sunday."

"I don't think so."

"Yeah. She did."

"Huh. That was weird."

"Her visit?"

"Her being here."

"Why?"

"She lives in New York."

"She did, yeah. She's been back for a year now."

He thought for a moment. "Mona always wanted that job."

"What job?"

"That magazine. The one you said. She used to say that to your mom. But the guy. He was never going to leave. And then he did."

That was twice today I'd now heard about the mysterious (at least to me) previous editor.

"Buddy Wheeler? Where did he go?"

"I don't know." He furrowed his brow. "But it was weird."

Then he paused, pondered, and then looked at me again. "So, where's the dog?"

I was saved by the arrival of the first of the dinner plates for the residents. I excused myself and walked the rest of the way back to the family house near Carmel Point. After dropping my things in the studio my dad built for me over the garage when I was in high school (giving us all some desperately needed space), I went down to the main house and saw Buster aka "the dog" and my Uncle Henry sitting in their usual spot in the family room next to the kitchen. As the sun set behind him, Uncle Henry — always distinguished his salt-and-pepper hair and black-rimmed glasses — was drinking his tea and reading one of his law journals, with bulldog Buster snoring beside him.

Before walking over to join them, I looked out at the bench in my late mom's succulent garden and beyond to the setting sun sitting just on top of the ocean. As always, I mentally thanked my great grandparents for choosing this gorgeous (and large by Carmel standards) spit of land near Carmel River State Beach to build their house. In

Chapter Two

those days, the area was considered the boondocks, based on the old picture hanging on the wall of their groundbreaking, which was surrounded by open space. While the lots around us had filled in and house itself changed a lot since then—the succulent garden my mom created was just one of the additions family members had made over the years—we still had one of the best views in town. This was especially true at sunset. Not that Henry noticed, with his nose in a book, as usual.

"Hey, Uncle Henry. Saw dad on my way home."

"How many times did he mention you didn't have the dog with you?"

"Two."

"Not bad then."

"Not bad at all. I'll bring Buster next time, although it might be a couple days as I have to go out to Carmel Valley and then to Big Sur on a new assignment."

"Fun."

"I don't know. They want me to work the magazine's bigger travel story on places in Monterey County for the issue they're centering around the Pebble Beach Pro-Am golf tournament."

"Makes sense."

"Booooring."

Henry looked at me over his glasses with a bemused smile. "Well, well, look at you, Miss Globetrotter. Too good for your own hometown?"

"It's not that. Well, maybe it is. I mean, come on, the trip starts at the golf resorts in the Carmel

Valley and ends at the golf resorts in Pebble Beach. Yawn."

"There's a lot in the middle there that you might be surprised to find."

As Uncle Henry was talking, I spotted a small blip moving across the water. That was odd. I grabbed the binoculars from the shelf and looked out and saw a guy on a dinghy making his way toward the shore.

"What do you think he's doing?" I asked.

Henry looked over his shoulder at the boat. "It's water, Sam. He's floating on it."

"But where is he going? There's no marina anywhere near here. Whaddya think? A spy heading to our shores? Come on, Uncle Henry. Where is your imagination?"

Henry managed to mix a laugh with a sigh in a way only he knew how. He looked over the top of his glasses at me. "When does this assignment start again?"

"Yeah, yeah." I watched as the boat pulled up all the way onto a protected part of the shore. The person got out and pulled it farther onto the sand. "So, Dad mentioned it was weird when the former editor-in-chief left *Carmel Today*."

"Buddy Wheeler?" Henry thought for a moment and shrugged. "I suppose it was a little strange."

"In what way?"

"Everybody thought he was going to go down with the ship—in his case the magazine. You know, be there until he keeled over one day at his

Chapter Two

desk or ran it into the ground, whichever came first. He was synonymous with *Carmel Today* for years. For good and for bad, I suppose. The last few years were pretty bad. He acted erratically and other local magazines were launched, which I'm sure hurt their ad sales. Then he up and resigned and the old owner, Hugh Tompkins, decided to sell."

"Tompkins wasn't going to sell before?"

"Not while Buddy was still there. I think they had some deal."

"Where did Buddy go, then?"

"I'm not sure. I remember your dad always felt it was a little funny the way Buddy up and left, but I don't think he ever uncovered anything suspicious. Or maybe he did. That was after he had retired from the force and the Alzheimer's was kicking in."

Henry paused for a second, acknowledging the guilt we both still felt at not having been able to handle his illness ourselves, before continuing: "Then Mona came home and took the magazine over for the new owners. After that, well, you came home, and I guess you know the rest."

I watched as the guy on the beach methodically took a bunch of fishing gear out of his boat and put it into a nearby van up on Seaview Drive. He then somehow balanced the small rubber boat on his back and got it up there as well. Huh. Guess he was just fishing, but it was the first time I'd seen anything like that around here.

※ Destination: Monterey ※

Okay, so maybe my dad wasn't the only one who looked for things that weren't there, and maybe there were new things for me to discover outside of my usual haunts. Perhaps taking a little time to tour around Monterey would allow me to see the area in a new light.

CHAPTER THREE

On Wednesday, as scheduled, I prepared to embark on my specially curated press trip through Monterey County. Even though I would be treading through familiar terrain, I decided to treat the trip as professionally as possible. It was my role as a travel writer to use my journalistic skills to look at all these places with a fresh eye, after all. With that in mind, after lunch I packed my overnight bag, left a note for Uncle Henry, patted Buster, got in my old, forest-green RAV-4—a beat-up car that was perfect for following crime stories in Los Angeles and a bit out of place in Carmel—and was off.

The first item on Chelsea's fancy itinerary was a visit to Carmel Valley. Just a dozen miles to the center of Carmel Valley Village from the coast, the valley was a world away in terms of terrain and personality. Where Carmel-by-the-Sea is, as its name suggests, surrounded by water, often encased in fog, and thus quite temperate (we rarely tipped past the 70-degree mark, even—or especially—in the summer), the valley could get quite warm. And while Carmel-by-the-Sea was a hilly hamlet crowded with trees, Carmel Valley featured wide-open agrarian terrain, its rolling hills filled with vineyards, ranches, and artisanal farms. It was also, as my first stop suggested, home to a number of golf resorts. Golf, ugh. Growing up a tennis player—and a public court tennis player at that—the golf types at the snooty country clubs and resorts where we played some of our junior tennis tournaments were never my favorite.

Open mind, Sam, open mind, I thought as, at 2 p.m. (right on schedule, I would like to note), I pulled off Carmel Valley Road and into the Carmel Valley Golf Lodge. I parked and checked in with reception before walking through the grounds of the sprawling complex to my room. When I entered, I found a note from the director of sales and marketing confirming our 3 p.m. appointment on the table next to the TV (the latest flat screen, of course). Next to the note was a packet filled with press releases and a little gift I had learned on my previous press trip was called an "amenity": a small basket filled with local products, including some olive oil, goat cheese, and a bottle of wine. Nice.

Chapter Three

According to the materials in both Chelsea's itinerary and the packet of press releases left with the amenity, the resort had recently refurbished their guest rooms in a design they called "golf resort chic." They upgraded the bedding with "Egyptian cotton linens" and added "luxurious granite and marble" to the bathrooms. I did a complete walk-through and took some photos for the website, and all of that was true, as far as I could see. Who am I to tell the difference between Egyptian cotton and any other kind of cotton?

I opened the curtains in my room to look outside—the materials touted a golf course view—and, yep, hello golf course. In case the view wasn't enough to remind me where I was, I heard a loud "thwack" and saw a golf ball soar past my room into the distance. Between the way the resort laid out the rooms and the large shade-providing oak trees that surrounded the patio, there was no danger of the ball hitting my deck (or closer), but I still decided to stay inside, at least for now. Besides, I had my appointment with the director of sales and marketing.

At a quarter of three, I started walking over to the lobby. As I did, I passed a tennis center—a rather large one, I thought, not to be mentioned at all in the resort's name—and paused to take a look at the people running right and left and front and back to hit the fuzzy yellow ball that had been such a big part of my childhood. As I pondered Lizzy's request to get back out on the court with her, I heard a familiar voice.

"Samantha Powers, is that you?"

I looked over to find an older man wearing a wide-brimmed hat using a large rolling contraption to scoop up tennis balls on the far end of the court.

"Mr. Tanaka?" Mr. Tanaka had been the tennis pro running the programs on the Carmel public courts when Lizzy and I were just starting to play as kids. He had the same huge grin on his face he always had when we were kids. I tried to figure out how old he might be because we thought he was ancient when we were kids and that was a good 25 years ago.

"In the flesh," he answered.

"When did you start working here?"

"Probably about the time you went off to college and Lizzy joined the tour."

"How do you like it?"

"The valley? It's great."

"I meant the resort."

"Oh, it's the best. I love it here. Top-notch courts and a good group of members with a batch of young kids to inspire, in addition to the resort guests. Speaking of which, what are you doing these days? I heard you were in Los Angeles writing about murder and mayhem."

"No. Well, I was. Now I'm writing about travel for *Carmel Today* magazine. I'm actually here to meet with the director of sales and marketing."

"Sounds like you got yourself a nice gig, too."

"It has its moments."

"How long have you been back?"

Chapter Three

"About five months."

"Yeah, I heard about your dad. Sorry."

Affecting as it did the former police chief in a relatively small community, my dad's diagnosis had spread pretty quickly. "Thanks, I appreciate that."

"Been hanging out with Lizzy?"

"I have. You?"

"Not as much as I would like. I tried to get her to join the staff here when she left the tour, but she wanted to start that darn pooch café instead."

"Guess she wanted her life to be about more than tennis."

"As you know, that is just crazy talk to me. I can't imagine a better life than being out here on the court every day running and jumping and hitting a tennis ball—or in my case these days, feeding tennis balls so others can run and jump and hit."

Again with the huge smile.

"I am happy that Lizzy's at least keeping her toe in the game with the help she's giving the team over at the public high school," Tanaka continued. "I told her she could bring them out here for special workouts once or twice a month. How about you, Sam? You playing?"

"Oh, Mr. Tanaka, I haven't picked up a racket in years."

"We're both adults now. You can call me Steve. And it's like riding a bike. The strokes come right back," he said. "You always had so much talent."

"Lizzy had all the talent."

"No, Lizzy had the competitive drive AND the talent. It's a rare combination to have both, which is why she did so well, but you had talent, too, Sam."

That was sweet, but obviously, the man had spent way too much time in the sun.

"Thanks, Steve." Wow, that felt weird to use his first name. "That's nice of you."

"It's true. Anytime you'd like to come out here and hit with me, you are welcome."

"Thanks. I appreciate that."

I did. Appreciate it.

Then I noticed some people playing a game on one of the outer courts that was definitely NOT tennis. They were using a much smaller footprint on the court and what appeared to be paddles and a whiffle ball that made a big "thwack" (not a golf ball thwack but more a plastic thwack so maybe more of a "clack"?).

"What's that?" I asked.

"Ugh. Pickleball."

"Pickleball?"

"Yep. People are mad about it—in every sense of the word. I've got half the club members who think it's the best thing since sliced bread—mostly the older ones whose knees aren't as spry as they used to be and like that the court is so much smaller—and half that want to ban it because of the noise the whiffleball makes when it hits the racket."

"The 'clack' sound?"

"I think of it more as a 'thwack.'"

Chapter Three

"See, I think the golf ball is the one that makes the 'thwack' sound."

Tanaka laughed. "Sam, that brain of yours always did get you in trouble. On the tennis court and off."

I laughed. "I suppose that's true."

"You know it."

"It was good seeing you," I said, and really meant it. "Good luck with everything."

"Hey, it's all cool," he said. "I'm still out here in the fresh air running and jumping and hitting, Sam."

Just then a middle-aged couple walked out onto the court for a lesson. They had the paunchy midsections and new clothing branded with the resort's logo that meant they were just taking up the game. "Let's see if I can keep these resort guests from joining the pickleballers, shall we?" Steve said. "Hey, it was really good seeing you, too, Sam. Don't be a stranger."

I continued on over to the reception area of the resort to meet the director of sales and marketing. She was hard to miss as she was the only one milling through the lobby wearing a suit and heels. Naturally, she immediately reminded me of Stacy (enough that I wondered if they were related and/or if all salespeople looked alike).

"Hello, Samantha. Nice to meet you. I'm Nadine," she said in such a rapid clip it made me feel like she was in a rush. "I'm so glad you were able to come and check out our renovations. It's been such an exciting project."

"The room is lovely."

"Isn't it? I was so glad to get rid of those old bedspreads and the burnt orange colors of the decor. The new design really brings the surrounding wine country into the golf resort aesthetic."

"Oh yes," I said, without really having any idea what she was talking about.

Nadine motioned me over to a waiting golf cart. "Why don't we tool around the grounds, and I can show you what else we've done?"

I had barely gotten my butt into my seat before she headed off at a speed that was at times concerning on a path that wound its way up and over hills and through the resort, which was much bigger than it looked at first.

"I left a press kit with all the stats on the renovation, so you don't have to write any of this down. In short, we spent about $5 million and really brought the Carmel Valley Golf Lodge up to the same level as the resorts over in Pebble Beach—not that we are competing," Nadine said, with a guffaw that kind of belied what she was saying as she took a left that had me tipping at a 45-degree angle and holding on for dear life.

"Plus," Nadine continued, "we have the added benefit of a warmer climate than Pebble, not to mention all the amazing wines that grow here in the valley due to the cool ocean air from the Pacific Coast blending with the warmth of the sun-drenched valley."

The way the line so closely mirrored the information found in the materials I had just read

Chapter Three

almost made me laugh. Obviously, Nadine had given this spiel before. I continued to hold on for dear life as we zipped around the grounds, and she rattled off stats on the renovations they had made to the rooms and the lobby and the clubhouse. Occasionally, she would screech to a stop so I could take some pictures on my iPhone before heading back out like she was part of the golf cart version of Le Mans.

Once the tour was over, Nadine dropped me at my room. She gave me her card and told me to call if I had any other questions before speeding off to her next pressing engagement before I could even finish thanking her for her time.

It was still early, so after regaining my equilibrium, drinking some of the sparkling water they'd left in the room to settle my stomach, and posting photos on the various *Carmel Today* sites, I figured I would head on over to Carmel Valley Village. This way, I would have time to walk around the area and check everything out before the evening's festivities started.

I found a parking space on the street that would allow me to easily walk the few blocks on either side of Carmel Valley Road that made up the village area. A quick perusal on the north side of the street identified a few restaurants, but mostly wine-tasting rooms. According to the materials, they represented just some of the 175 vineyards in the Monterey County wine growing area. The majority grew the ever-popular pinot and chardonnay grapes, which thrived in the cool ocean air hitting the warm valley that Nadine had described, but the microclimates in certain areas allowed more than 40 other varietals to be grown as well.

Interesting stuff, but I didn't want to do any official tastings, and to be honest, had no idea which of the wineries I might choose. I walked in and out of a few to see how their personalities were reflected before crossing from the north to the south side of the street. There, I discovered more tasting rooms, but also art galleries, a book boutique, glass blowing demonstrations, and a small market that carried local products. I have to admit these were all things I didn't remember being there before. Not that I had ever really walked around the area the way a tourist would, I suppose. Maybe there was more to discover than I anticipated, and this wasn't such a bad idea after all.

Maybe.

CHAPTER FOUR

Not wanting to lose track of time, I looked at my watch. It was 5:50, so I walked down the street and found the tasting room for the Robert O. Carpenter (or R.O.C. on the sign) Winery. It was part of an indoor-outdoor complex that also contained what looked to be an artisanal farm goods shop, an art gallery, and a small-but-fun-looking bar called "HANGOUT." A lit-up fountain highlighted a courtyard in the middle of it all. It wasn't hard to figure out which of the entities was hosting the reception as someone had staged a large poster version of the current *Carmel Today* cover just outside R.O.C. Winery's front door, which separated a front patio area from the indoor tasting room. The patio was already filled with people, including staffers that included Toupee Tom and Tottering Terry.

It was interesting to see Tom outside of his normal environment in the editorial pod at the *Carmel Today* offices. He actually looked happier, wearing a much lighter expression on his face than the usual beleaguered grimace. Dare I say it? The corners of Tom's mouth were even turned up into something resembling a smile as he laughed at something Terry was saying. The two of them were surrounded by a group of people in their age bracket. As I mentioned, part of the reason Mona had kept them both on at the magazine was the cachet they gave her with the old school Carmelites she had lost touch with when she moved to New York. I felt like I was viewing the two of them in their natural habitat for the first time.

I waved and Tom nodded and tipped his drink at me. I didn't stop to chat, deciding to continue on into the tasting room instead. Younger than that outdoor crowd by a few decades, I really didn't want to be the novelty addition. Plus, even though Tom and Terry were part of the group, they all gave off the feeling of a high school clique where I didn't totally belong.

You're not in high school anymore, Sam, I thought. *You are an accomplished investigative reporter who is now a globetrotting (well, one trip, but still) travel writer and you are here in that role.* With that in mind, I stood up a little straighter and entered the tasting room itself. I took stock of the surroundings. So far, it was pretty much your typical wine-industry fare: large glossy photographs

Chapter Four

of vineyards lined the walls along with stylish wine racks filled with dozens and dozens of bottles. Various types of glassware to pair with the particular varietals were stationed on the bar, where a few young black-clad wine pourers were pouring away under the direction of a small and very energetic-looking woman. She appeared to be in her 40s, had straight brown hair cut very short, and wore a nicer black top with the logo of the winery on the pocket as she explained the intricacies of each wine to the people at the bar.

Also included in the room were a small gift shop and a number of high-top tables, where appetizer-bearing servers mingled among the people. In the back, I could see the area that had undergone an expansion. It looked like they had knocked out the back wall to create space for a bandstand. It sat next to an accordion-style glass door that opened up to another outdoor patio.

Luckily, I immediately spotted Mona to help me break the ice. Her extreme height was always a blessing at these types of events. She waved me over to the far corner of the bar, where the bottles of R.O.C. wine were lined up. From what I could see, there were the requisite chardonnay and pinot noir, plus a syrah, a rosé, and a viognier. Iconoclast that I am, I asked for a glass of the viognier and joined Mona, who was deep in conversation with a middle-aged couple who looked like they stepped right out of the pages of *Town & Country* magazine. The man wore a polo-style shirt and khakis, and he had a cashmere sweater tied around his neck to go with shellacked Ken-doll-brown hair that I'm sure was dyed, but I have to admit was a damn good job. He was standing next to a striking woman with long wavy dark brown hair that had impeccable highlights. Made me wonder if their colorist made house calls.

"Samantha, I'm so glad you are here," said Mona, whose ability to mingle with any- and everyone she met was a skill set I had yet to acquire. Naturally, she was perfectly dressed for the occasion in a tailored pantsuit accentuated with a necklace dangling dark purple glass beads that from afar resembled grapes.

"Samantha Powers, this is Robert..." Mona said, referring to the sweater dude. "...and Barbara Carpenter. And their dog Bruno."

I looked down at a huge Bull Mastiff sporting a scarf with the *Carmel Today* logo sitting next to petite little Cornwall wearing the same scarf. Nice touch.

"As you know, Bob and Barb are the new owners of *Carmel Today* magazine."

"It's so nice to meet you," I said, holding out my hand. "I love your dog's attire."

"Fabulous, isn't it? We've been brainstorming with Mona here on new *Carmel Today* logo items we might create," said Barb. "Naturally, we had to start with the dog scarves."

"Well, of course." I mean, in Carmel, that was understood, right?

"It's so nice to meet you, Samantha," Barb said, looking me straight in the eye and shaking my

Chapter Four

hand and giving her hair an impressive (especially for those of us with locks on the curly side that do not) flip.

Bob nodded from his position next to her, doing none of the above.

"You can call me Sam."

"Of course—and as Mona mentioned, everybody just calls us Bob and Barb." Barb gave me a warm smile, and I immediately liked her, even if I still envied the hair flipping thing.

"I love your winery."

"Wine-tasting room," Bob corrected me. Okay, so, I immediately *didn't* like him.

"The actual winery is near our vineyards in the Santa Lucia Highlands AVA," he said, still not even looking directly at me.

"Oh, don't listen to him," Barb said with a loud laugh. "He's being a pompous bore because he would rather be home watching the game."

Bob nodded with nary a smile in sight. "I'm really regretting not putting TVs in this place."

"Powers. Powers…" Barb said. "Any relation to Carmel's former police chief Powers?"

"That's my dad."

"Whatever happened to him? He kind of disappeared from the scene."

"He's in a memory care center now with Alzheimer's-related dementia."

"Oh, honey, I'm so sorry to hear that," said Barb with a warm touch of my sleeve. "I can relate. I went through something similar with my mom."

"Thanks. I appreciate that."

"Is that why you came back to Carmel?"

I nodded.

"Well, I suppose then, at least for us, there is a silver lining. I—we—are so happy you have joined the magazine."

"It's pretty new, you owning the magazine, correct?"

"Very new. It's something we," she said, pointing to Bob, who now appeared to be watching the game on his iPhone, "had always wanted and finally made happen last year."

"I'm curious. What was the draw?"

"What a wonderful question," Barb said, again giving my arm a little touch. "It's the investigative reporter in you, isn't it?"

I shrugged and smiled. I mean, I was really just curious. I looked at Mona, who shrugged and smiled back.

"Well," Barb continued, "I guess it's because I used to work in magazines myself when I was right out of college and living in New York. In fact, I had a brief stint working for Mona at Condé Nast before moving back to San Francisco to be the managing editor for *Pacific Heights Living*. That's where I met Bob."

Bob gave the smallest wave possible with his hand while Barb continued. "Bob's family has always had properties here in the Carmel area—with the hotel and the restaurant back in town. After adding the winery and tasting room here in the valley, we started making this our primary

Chapter Four

home, and it became a dream of mine—ours, of course—to own the magazine."

"Someone told me the former owner wasn't interested in selling."

"Oh, he wasn't for a very long time. That was especially true when Buddy was running it—into the ground if you ask me. You should have seen some of the stories he was running. But Hugh..."

"Hugh?"

"Hugh Tompkins, the previous owner. We're members of the same club and have known him forever, of course. Hugh was always definitive about a sale never happening. Then after hearing that Buddy was thinking of retiring, we ran into Hugh. I mentioned again how much we loved the magazine and Hugh said he might now consider selling. Bob asked him to name his price, he did, and well, here we are!" she said, waving to the scene in the wine-tasting room.

"I loved your story on the Mokihana Resort, by the way," Barb continued, again giving my arm a little touch. "Bob and I just booked a stay there for the holidays."

I touched the leather bracelet Roger Kai gave me in Hawaii. It had a spiral clasp carved out of bone that Roger said meant new beginnings. *Newer every day, Rog. Newer every day.*

"I'm so glad to hear. It really is a wonderful resort," I said.

"And now here you are covering our new music venue!" Barb said, happily waving toward the scene in the wine-tasting room, which was starting to fill up with more people as the band was setting up behind them. "We'll also be able to host comedy or trivia and other fun entertainment options."

"The opening of a new cultural venue is a boon to the area," Stiletto Stacy said, walking in from the back patio to join us wearing some seriously pointy shoes. I swear, with her ability to balance on those sticks, the woman could get a job in a circus act or, I suppose, do some real damage in a dark alley with a Buffy kick. "It's exactly the kind of thing we like to cover in the magazine!"

Stacy and Barb did the air kiss thing, and Stacy gave a little wave to Bob, who nodded imperceptibly. Wow. The guy really had zero social skills or even personality that I could see. Hard to figure out what drew such a gregarious person like Barb to him except the obvious (money, of course).

"Thank you so much for promoting the magazine at this event, Barb," Stacy said.

"But of course," said Barb.

"Synergy!" they both said before laughing hysterically. Mona looked over with an enigmatic smile that befitted her namesake in the Louvre as she watched Stacy and Barb chat away like the old friends that they were. It was times like these that I had a hard time knowing what Mona was thinking.

"Naturally, I would love to get a quote from you—or Bob—about the addition of the venue beyond what we got in the press release," I

Chapter Four

said when Barb and Stacy took a break from their chatting.

"Of course, my dear, I'd be happy to," Barb said. Then she looked behind me, lit up, and called out, "Chelsea! Over here."

Oh, great. FU Chelsea makes her appearance. And I have to say, it was quite an appearance. Gone were the boots and jacket of her "professional personal branding," and in its place what I suppose was the "cocktail party" version. She had her long blond hair cascading down around her shoulders and wore a little black dress with one of the deepest v-necks I'd ever seen. Made me wonder what kind of double-sided tape she was using to make sure the girls didn't come flopping out unexpectedly. As Chelsea walked—strutted, really—over to us on seriously high platform shoes, she flipped her hair back and forth like a model in a shampoo commercial. Chelsea made a beeline toward her fellow hair-flipper Barb in a way that made it clear that Barb, not Bob (who gave a quick nod from the bar) was the blood relative.

"Auntie Barb!" Chelsea gave Barb a big hug, gave Bob a smaller and very awkward hug, and dog Bruno a pat on the head.

"I'm so glad you made it."

"Of course! I can't wait to see what you've done with the space," Chelsea said before turning to me and saying, "I hope you got a quote from them for the story, Sam."

Before I could smack the top of her head (I was happy to still be a few inches taller than Chelsea even in her platform shoes), Barb laughed. "Oh, Chelsea, have a glass of wine before you start dictating to everybody. Besides, it's not long before the music is going to begin, and our guest of honor appears."

"Who's that?"

"Michael MacLean, of course," Barb said as if I was supposed to know who that was. "Only the three-time winner of the Pebble Beach Pro-Am, among other tournaments. He just started playing on the Champions tour but still plays the pro-am with some of the other veteran players on a PGA exemption."

"Champions tour?"

"It's for golfers over 50," Stacy offered.

"Michael's a local boy," Barb said. "So he always gets invited to play—and he is going to be our cover subject, right Mona?"

"Yes, I interviewed him earlier today and the photoshoot is set for tomorrow."

"Oh, and speak of the devil: there he is."

Everyone turned toward the door, and for the first time, even Bob came to life.

And there we were: back to golf. Ugh.

CHAPTER FIVE

The sea of people at the door parted as Michael MacLean made his way through the crowd. He spotted Mona, nodded, and started making his way over to her. He cut a striking figure—I will give him that. Tall, with piercing blue eyes, and sporting a few gray highlights in his dark brown hair, he was really quite handsome—if a good 15 years older than I was and someone who had gotten way too much sun for his own good. When he reached Mona, people started gathering around a little too close for my comfort. I started backing out of the scrum.

I walked over toward the part of the room where the band was finishing setting up. When I turned back, I found Chelsea right behind me. Her gaze moved past me in the direction I had been looking, but instead of the bandstand, she was staring directly at a guy standing in a group of people next to it holding a glass of red wine. Based on his looks—about my mid-30s age and trying a little too hard for the bohemian look with his studiously tousled dark brown hair, three-day scruff, and baggy jacket—I'm going to guess it was the pinot and not the syrah he was holding. Or maybe it was the other way around, depending on how hard he was working to be a nonconformist. Hard to say. He wasn't bad looking, I will say that. No, even if his look was a bit affected, he was mighty fine on the eyes. Aesthetically speaking, of course.

"You see him, don't you?" Chelsea said, suddenly closer to my side.

"See who?"

"Him!" Chelsea pointed at the bohemian dude next to the band.

"Is he in the band?"

"Uh, no, Sam. He's not," Chelsea said, in a snotty tone that again made me want to thwack (clack?) her on the head.

"I take it you know him."

"Of course, I know him. Don't you?"

"I do not."

"Oh, Sam. You are so out of it."

"I am, Chelsea. Quite out of it."

"That's Brody Montgomery."

"And he is?"

"Brody Montgomery? The photographer? His mom is married to Uncle Bob's best friend, so I have hung out with him a bit."

Chapter Five

The girl was absolutely swooning as she continued. "See, Brody grew up here in Big Sur and takes *amazing* photographs of the area—well, like that one," Chelsea said, pointing to some of the pictures of the vineyards that hung on the wall back where the high tops were and to some pretty dramatic scenes of waves crashing against Big Sur cliffs in the music venue. "Uncle Bob commissioned a few more for his hotel and restaurant."

"Cool."

"Oh, Sam, it's beyond cool. Beyond cool—as is he, but of course, you can see that, can't you?"

I had never seen this side of her. She was absolutely cooing while also somehow chastising me in her typical sanctimonious tone for not knowing this dude.

"Do you want to go talk to him?" I asked.

"Only if you will go with me."

Not sure why she was suddenly shy, but I said, "Uh, okay, sure." I looked over at Mona, who was still caught in the middle of the golfer dude scrum. I nodded toward Chelsea and then the guy in the corner and then shrugged. She returned my shrug and then turned back in the direction of the group surrounding her. Chelsea and I walked over toward the stage where Mr. Wonderful, or at least, Mr. Thinks He's Wonderful (based on his swagger) was standing.

We walked over to the band area. I nodded to the bassist and wondered, as I often do, why they never seem to have any hips. I mean, seriously, maybe we could take up a collection and buy the man a cheeseburger, or a dozen. I turned back to find Chelsea flipping her hair back dramatically as she chatted with Brody Montgomery.

"We're here covering the opening of the music venue for *Carmel Today*, of course," Chelsea said, before noticing I was standing there. "This is Samantha, our reporter."

Our reporter? Really, Chelsea?

"You have a reporter?" Brody asked.

"Meaning?" Chelsea asked in an annoyed tone.

"Not sure how much reporting is required for the stuff they run in *Carmel Today*," he said rather dismissively.

Chelsea turned beet red. Not sure why, since it was me he was dissing, although I guess it was the whole magazine he was dissing.

"Nice to know the guy who takes pictures of vines is also a media critic," I said.

"Ha—she got you," the tiny gal with short straight brown hair I saw earlier explaining the wines behind the bar piped up. "Don't listen to him, Samantha. He thinks he's better than everybody ever since he sold a picture of the Big Sur fire last year to *National Geographic*."

"I've sold quite a few photos now, quite a few," Brody said, a little too quickly.

"Only because you happened to be in the right place at the right time—and used my vine drone to get them," she said. "The rest have all been all to your mom's husband's friend." Okay, I loved her, too.

Chapter Five

"I didn't get your name?" I asked my new best friend. (Sorry, Lizzy, make room for a new best friend.)

"I'm Jen. I'm actually the winemaker for the Carpenters—sorry, R.O.C."

"You made this? It's quite good," I said. And I wasn't lying. Not to sound like a snob, but I'd long been a fan of wines made from viognier grapes—which weren't easy to find in the Monterey area, with its fondness for chardonnay—and this was a really good one.

"Thanks! We found a plot of land where the viognier really thrive. They're organically grown, too. If you only knew how hard I had to fight Bob on that when he asked me to take over the winery. I made him put it in the contract when he hired me away from my former winery in the Carneros region of Napa."

"Napa. Fancy."

"You know it. Gave me the vine cred I needed to get what I wanted from Bob, I'll tell you that."

Really, she was a kick.

"How long have you been with the winery?" I asked.

"A little over three years. Came on not long after Bob bought it. The previous owners did some great things but also some not-so-great things. The changes we are making take time, but the vines are solid, and we're making progress now that Bob's on board."

"What's his deal? He doesn't seem to be the most social guy, especially compared to Barb."

"Right? He's not a bad guy—just your typical entitled straight white rich dude—but he's competitive and wants to create the best wines so he can boast about them to his friends at the club. That gives me leverage to move him in the right direction. If that doesn't work, I will admit I have on occasion gone through Barb when I really needed something. She's definitely more accessible."

Just then another woman came up wearing a long linen tunic over black leggings and sandals. "Hey, do you know Holly?" Jen said. "She runs Riverside Farms. She was one of my TAs when I was in the ag program at UC Davis many moons ago."

Holly was a little older than Jen—maybe in her early 50s. She had tousled curls like mine but longer and strawberry blond and mixed with silver strands that framed a sun-dappled face.

"I don't. Nice to meet you, Holly. I'm Sam, a writer for *Carmel Today*," I said, looking over at Brody and Chelsea, both of whom looked to be fuming away.

"*Carmel Today*? Cool! You guys did such a nice piece on us when we first took over the farm ten years ago," said Holly.

"Good to hear. Who was the writer on that piece?" I have to admit my curiosity as to the workings of *Carmel Today* magazine before I got there had only been increasing.

"Jason Rhodes. Very young. Right out of college, I think. From what Jason said when he came

Chapter Five

out to interview us, the old editor-in-chief used to kind of cycle through young writers. But like I said, this kid did a really nice job, and we got a bunch of new clients off the publicity."

"I'm glad to hear. What do you grow?"

"Lavender, mostly. It loves it out here in the valley. We turn it into all sorts of products or, really, partner with friends of ours who make it into all sorts of products—soap, lotion, essential oils, you name it. My partner and I also have beehives—because bees love lavender so why not?—and some chickens. And we rent part of our space to a goat cheesemaker. He's the one who started the farm and then sold it to us with the caveat that he gets to stay on with his goats. He's a font of information on how best to work that land, so it works out for all of us."

"How cool!" I said and really meant it. Both Holly and Jen were so obviously passionate about their work that it radiated through their faces as pure joy. Made me wonder if I would ever have a job that made me look like that.

"Yeah, it is pretty cool. The land that we use up backs up to the river near Palo Colorado Canyon—hence the Riverside name. It's pretty rugged, but the goats are happy up in those hills, and we've made the rest of the land work with what we're doing. We're able to sell everything we make either to our friends or to the resorts and shops in Carmel and Big Sur, so we don't have to deal with distributors or worry about shipping or any of the other retail concerns."

"Again, I have to say that's so cool," I said.

Holly smiled and nodded. I could see she was proud of what she had accomplished. Just as I was about to ask her more about it, the music started. It was a very earnest-looking light jazz trio that the older folks in the crowd were really enjoying. Not really my scene but, heck, if I was honest, I was still figuring out my scene.

As more of the outdoor crowd started moving inside—again creating conditions that bordered on claustrophobic (at least for me)—Jen gestured to me and Holly, and the three of us started a slow walk back toward the front door.

"What do you think about heading over to Bowie's?" Jen asked.

Holly smiled, nodded, and looked at me.

"It's just across the courtyard," Holly said. I nodded as well. Whatever that was sounded good to me. I looked over and noticed Chelsea was deep in conversation with Brody over in the corner. There was more hair flipping involved, as well as Barb's technique of a light touch on the arm to indicate warmth, so I figured I would just keep doing the slow walk back out the door with the others. I had gotten plenty of material on the new venue for the "Out and About" story, and it would be good to include the other entities in the courtyard as part of the Carmel Valley nightlife options in the bigger "road to the Pebble Beach Pro-Am" story. Besides, it was nice to finally meet some people closer to my own age who weren't

Chapter Five

the typical golf club types like most of those gathered inside.

We made our way across the courtyard to the small bar with the "HANGOUT" sign that I had noticed earlier. It was actually, as I was instructed, a "cidery," a cute way to refer to a place that specializes in ciders vs. beers or wine, although those were offered as well. The place was decked out with couches and tables filled with all sorts of games. Jen pointed to two couches in the corner, and we headed over there.

A young guy with a buzz cut and some serious tattoos on his arms came up. "Hey there, how's it going?"

"It's going, Bowie. It's going," said Jen.

"This is our new friend, Sam," said Holly, pointing at me.

I waved and Bowie waved back. "This place is great," I said, and I meant it. Who knew there was somewhere like this out here? Not me, that's who.

"Thanks!" Bowie said. "When I got out of the military, I heard this space was available, and I figured it might be fun to try something a little different. So far, so good, right?"

"So far, so great," Holly said. "Truth be told, Bowie's my son, Sam." Bowie gave a big ole grin, and I could see the resemblance. "And, yes, before you ask, the son of two organic farmers went into the military."

"I wanted to jump out of planes," he said with a wry smile.

"And did you?"

"I did. When I was ready to come home, mom and dad helped me find this space."

"Actually, Jen helped us with that."

"I just hooked them up with Bob. He—well, his family—owns this whole complex," Jen said. "Bowie presented his idea for this small space and Bob loved it. Gave him a good deal for the first few years while the place gets on its feet."

Bob? Middle-aged Ken-doll Bob? The one currently with his nose in his phone watching a football game? I found it surprising that someone so old school in appearance and, for lack of a better word, manners would be open to trying all the new things Jen kept mentioning. I mean, organic winery, music venue, and now a cidery? Even the art gallery I'd passed when I walked around the complex earlier looked more on the avant-garde side than the big expensive paintings at the galleries in town.

"I can see your brain ticking away, Sam," said Jen. "Like I said, appearances aside, Bob is a competitive guy—especially since he met Barb, who has polished him up quite a bit, as you can imagine."

I laughed at the fact my face was giving me away (again). "He cleans up well, I guess."

"Ha—yes. They've got a lot to prove to that family of his in San Francisco. Part of the reason they moved down here. Gave them a bit more latitude in their business ventures. Bob and Barb did a great job updating the hotel and the restaurant in town. The stuff they're doing out here in

Chapter Five

the valley—renovating this lot and bringing in some new concepts based on things they've seen elsewhere, like letting Bowie open this cidery—is pretty cool."

"Looks like so far the cidery has been a hit."

"We're doing okay," Bowie said, smiling. "It's been fun. I'll bring you all tastes of some new ciders we just got in."

Holly beamed like the proud mom she was, and Jen started bobbing her head to the music playing in the background as Bowie started moving off to another table. He passed Brody making a beeline for our table.

"Brody, my boy," said Jen. "Have a seat."

"I'm actually going to take off. Long drive back to Big Sur," said Brody, nodding at me and offering a smile that I am going to admit was not unwelcome. Like I said, the boy was not bad on the eyes.

"Makes sense. Drive safe," said Jen. "Those roads can be tough at night."

My stomach lurched a little as I pushed down a memory I really didn't want to revisit.

Brody nodded. "Don't worry, Jen. I grew up on those roads." He turned to me. "Bye, Sam. It was really nice meeting you!"

Brody took my hand and clasped it with the other hand. A cheesy move, but not without its merits. He then looked over his shoulder with a slightly panicked look and ducked out the open door in the back. Soon, Chelsea was heading toward our table and looking around for (I'm guessing) a Brody that had already departed.

"Well, hello, Sam," she said in a snotty voice. "What are you doing here?"

"Uh, hanging with Jen and Holly?"

"Shouldn't you still be covering the Carpenter's event?"

"Uh, no. I got what I needed for that story and think we have plenty of representation over there."

Chelsea looked for a brief moment like she was going to say something else. Instead, she harrumphed, turned on her heels and headed toward the front door—where, for a second, I thought I saw Michael MacLean watching from just outside—before turning back and saying, "We'll talk at the gallery opening tomorrow afternoon."

"Uh, okaaaaay."

Chelsea then finished her stalking out of the door while Holly and Jen snickered next to me. I couldn't tell if MacLean was still in the doorway or not.

"I can't believe you have to work for her..." Jen said.

"WITH, WITH her, not for her, thank goodness."

"Still. Wow."

"Yeah. Wow is right."

Jen, who was one of those types of people who probably never sat still, said, "So, what do you think? Should we get this Jenga set up?"

"Let's do it..."

CHAPTER SIX

The next day, after posting my event photos on the sites, I checked out of my room at the Carmel Valley Golf Lodge and headed down to Big Sur. As I drove, I thought about the fun I'd had the night before at "HANGOUT" with Jen and Holly. The games, the laughing. Really, it was the first time I'd done anything like that since I got home. Truth be told, except for my trip to Maui, it was the first time I had done anything fun in years. The last couple of years in Los Angeles, my life revolved around a job covering the worst in humanity while dealing with a truly dysfunctional relationship that I tried ending multiple times before finally doing it for good when I left to return home.

But last night, that was, well, just plain old fun. The residual feeling it brought gave me a bit of a lift as I headed back toward the coast on Carmel Valley Road. When I reached Highway 1, I turned left and started to make my way south toward Big Sur, where the area's famous winding roads featured rocky cliffs dropping down to the Pacific Ocean on my right and verdant hills leading up into the Santa Lucias mountains on my left. It was a drive I always found a little nerve-wracking and hadn't done since my mom's accident, so I was happy to be making it during the day.

I followed the directions to the hotel that I had loaded onto my GPS. Even though there was just one main road in and I had grown up nearby, it felt necessary to use GPS because the various spots along Highway 1 that constituted "Big Sur" tended to pop up suddenly around a bend, and I wanted to know when to start slowing up. That's the thing about Big Sur: there's no real center or "town." Instead, a number of small enclaves offering lodging, restaurants, stores, and other entities pop up occasionally along the approximately 75-mile coastline running between Carmel in the north and San Simeon in the south. To make things even more confusing, it's not even all in one county—with the northern parts in Monterey County and the southern in San Luis Obispo—and parts are so rugged that there is (even in this day and age) no cell phone reception.

As I headed down the coast on Highway 1, the terrain included a mix of roads built precariously into the side of the mountain, over bridges crossing deep gulches, through impossibly tall

Chapter Six

trees that blocked light from getting through, and crossing flat verdant pastures. At one of those flatter junctures, I saw a deer—idiots that they are (sorry, Bambi)—meandering across the road up ahead of me. I pulled over to the right onto a patch of driveway to give the deer a chance to make it all the way across the road and make sure it didn't change its mind and quickly dart back across, as they have been known to do.

As I waited, I noticed that the driveway where I pulled over was part of the entrance to a private property that—in case I wasn't sure—was designated as such by a big rope between two fence posts hoisting a "Private Property Do Not Enter" sign. I looked down to my right (the ocean side) and noticed that just before the lane heading down into the private property was a pretty steep drop-off. While it wasn't the cliffs-of-insanity that I would find later in the drive, I still wouldn't want to be going over the side of it anytime soon.

Once the deer made it safely across, I continued on. I passed a few places where Holly mentioned she would be making deliveries for her farm cooperative. It reminded me that she said she was also dropping off some products at the inn where I was staying and that I was welcome to come along on some of her other deliveries as a way to check out the area. The only concrete things on my itinerary were to check-in to the inn and have lunch in the restaurant with the new chef before attending the art gallery reception later in the afternoon, so if she offered again, I planned on taking her up on it.

On paper—aka the itinerary Chelsea made up and a quick look at their website before I left—the hotel where I would be staying looked really cute. In general, Big Sur properties tended to run from the very primitive (camping) to the very luxurious (swank hotels) to the very quirky (yurts and even a monastery). There were also a few older motels and inns that ran the gamut between primitive and less primitive. The less primitive tended to have been purchased in recent years and upgraded by intrepid souls. I say intrepid because running a business in this more isolated part of the county meant dealing with issues from fires to floods and rockslides that can take out roads and bridges on a moment's notice. Slides along Highway 1 have been known to cut off access for weeks or even months on end, which obviously can make getting supplies—and guests—in and out rather difficult.

Today, I was checking out one of those renovated inns. Mona had told me that, while the luxurious lodgings found at hotels like Post Ranch Inn and Ventana were more well known and frequented by the crowd that read *Carmel Today*, these newer entries to the market had become a big draw for the "young affluent" looking for a more adventurous choice—a demographic they were desperately trying to attract as new readers of the magazine.

Chapter Six

According to the story *Carmel Today* ran the previous year (also conveniently included in my packet), the Wildflower Inn had been bought and renovated by a Bay Area couple. A designer and an architect, they made upgrades to the property that were both aesthetically pleasing and environmentally sustainable. More recently, they had reopened the inn's restaurant, which was headed up by a young chef who was only using local products in a menu he created daily. This made it a good time for us to check the place out again for those "young affluents" Mona had mentioned. Again, so far, this was all just according to the press materials that Mona, Chelsea, and the tourism bureau folks had provided. I would be the eyes and ears and taste buds that would decide if they had pulled it off. When we were at the cidery, Holly and Jen told me they knew the owners and the chef. They said they liked them a lot and that I would have a great time. Since in the short time I'd known them, they had not steered me wrong, I was really looking forward to it.

When the GPS did its little "destination on the right," I pulled over and got out. The inn was adjacent to a small complex that also included a store, a separate standalone restaurant and bar, and a gas station—offering gas at $1 more per gallon than back in Carmel, I noted (happy I had topped off in town). As I went to check-in, I took a few pictures of the exterior on my iPhone to post on the sites. The bones of the place were still old Big Sur, with a row of about ten wood-clad cabins adjacent to a building that served as the lodge and restaurant. I could immediately see the buildings had been spruced up while still staying within the original aesthetic. In a way, it reminded me of our family home. While originally built by my great grandparents, over the years each generation had added their own touches and updates. In my mom's case, that had been most felt in the garden, so I took note of and especially appreciated the lovely wildflower gardens that gave the inn its name as I opened the door to the main lodge.

Unlike the Carmel Valley Golf Lodge, I was not met by a suit-wearing director of sales and marketing wielding a golf cart, but by a couple who looked like they could have graced the cover of a magazine called *Bohemian Chic* (assuming one existed). Like Jen and Holly, they looked to be in their 40s or early 50s, and maybe I was reaching, but the image that first came to mind was of a couple that had lived and worked as professionals in the city before returning to the land of the oaks and redwoods. In other words, they fit the Hallmark Christmas Movie trope of a couple that returns to their roots to find themselves (sans the tacky holiday decorations). The woman had her long straight black hair pulled up into a bun with chopsticks. The man wore a plaid flannel shirt and a tool belt wrapped around his waist that he was reaching into as he repaired a bit of the wainscoting at the far end of the lobby. I pictured a meet-cute for the two of them at a

Chapter Six

home improvement store in the city or perhaps bumping into each other as they both looked at the same "Big Sur inn for sale" picture in a real estate window.

"It's so nice to meet you," the woman said as I entered. "My name is Naomi, and this is Evan."

"Nice to meet you both. I'm Sam from *Carmel Today*," I said, waving to Evan and taking in the surroundings, which were all just cute as a button. From the fresh flowers on the reception desk to the bookcases filled with books and board games to the note on the wall letting guests know about the lack of communications devices in the room — no phones, no TVs, etc. — the place screamed: "Relax already!"

"Sam! I'm so happy you made it," said Naomi with a huge smile. "I hope you are hungry as Chef Kiwan has an amazing meal prepared for you."

After I put my bag in my little cabin, which was just as adorable as the lodge, I met Naomi in the restaurant. It had about a dozen tables, which were somewhat irrelevant as I was the only person there. With big smiles, Naomi and Chef Kiwan, seemingly representing the one Black friend every good Hallmark Christmas movie provides, began bringing out tastes of the dishes they planned to feature on the menu, all of which were quite delicious.

I dutifully photographed each of the small courses Chef Kiwan, who was tall and had long black dreadlocks tied up in a bun not unlike the one Naomi wore, brought out. He would deposit each dish on the table with a huge grin on his face and then watch eagerly until I took the first bite and gave it a big thumbs-up. I wasn't acting. The food was amazing—from a fresh beet-and-goat-cheese carpaccio to a tuna tartare (sustainably caught, of course) to an egg custard that the chef had managed to place back into the original shell without cracking it. Still, it was a little uncomfortable being under the microscope (as it were), so I was happy when I saw Holly carrying a load of egg cartons into the kitchen.

"Holly!" I called out.

Holly dropped the cartons on the counter and came over to the table.

"Sam! How's it going?"

"Great! This lunch is incredible. Want to join me? There's way more than I can eat on my own, and I'd love the company."

Holly looked at her watch. "Sure! I'm not expected at Esalen until 2 o'clock anyway." Holly went back into the kitchen. "Hey, Chef Kiwan, can you bring an extra plate and a set of utensils so I can taste some of these amazing dishes you're creating?"

"HAPPY TO!" Chef Kiwan shouted and then bounded out with the plate and utensils, still with the huge grin on his face.

Holly took a bite. "Oh, Kiwan, you are a magician. This is amazing."

"It's all in the products, Holly."

"Hey, I eat some of these products every day, and they don't taste like this."

Chapter Six

"I can give you some pointers."

"That would be amazing."

What can I say? They were all so sweet and encouraging of each other, I could feel my innate cynicism start to melt.

"Sam," Holly said, pausing to give a little moan of happiness after one of the tastes, "as I mentioned last night, you should come with me as I make my stops along the coast to drop off products from the farms up in Carmel Valley. All I have left today are Nepenthe and Esalen."

I waited a polite two seconds before taking her up on it. I had a free afternoon, it was a beautiful day, and a little adventure sounded fun. Besides, it would give me fodder for my story, it wasn't a drive I liked making on my own, and there was an earth-mother quality to Holly that made me feel really comfortable with her, even though we had only just met.

When we were done with lunch and I had posted photos of the meal on the sites using the Wifi in the lodge, I profusely thanked the beaming chef and owners and jumped in Holly's truck, and we headed down the coast.

"Sorry about all the dog hair on the seat," said Holly. "We have these Great Pyrenees to guard the chickens and goats from predators. They're wonderful but shed up a storm."

I laughed. "Dog hair is a given in this area," I said. "My uncle has had a series of English bulldogs and bulldog mixes ever since he went to Yale law school, so I'm used to constantly brushing hair off myself."

Now Holly laughed. "Good to hear."

As we headed down Highway 1, Holly took the twists and turns like a pro, but I have to admit I started to get more freaked out than I would have liked. It never occurred to me how much scarier it would be to ride in the passenger seat, especially heading south. Not only do you lose the semblance of control you have when driving yourself, but seeing the cliffs drop off just inches from my door was a little unnerving. There were guard rails but also spots where they didn't exist, or worse, had crumbled because someone went through them (I'm assuming).

Holly, oblivious to my terror, kept chatting away. I gripped the door panel as my hands sweated. Occasionally, as she hit a corner, I inadvertently pushed the invisible brake beneath my foot.

"You okay?" Holly finally asked.

"These roads freak me out a little."

"Don't worry. I've driven them a million times. Haven't you? You grew up around here, didn't you?"

"I did. And it's not you I worry about. It's other people."

"There are the occasional loons on the road, but luckily not mid-week, especially this time of year."

"I know, it's just, well, I don't usually talk about this much, or really, ever, but my mom

Chapter Six

died on this road. Not here. Much farther down near Gorda."

There. I'd said it. The way my mom died was something I'd pushed down so far in the ten years since it happened that it felt alien to say it out loud. I immediately tried to quell the memory of getting the call from my dad—the only time I had ever heard him cry.

"Oh my god. Sam. I am so sorry."

"Thanks." I realized that while I had been lamenting everybody I came into contact with asking about my dad and his condition, what I missed was anyone talking about my mom. After ten years of her being gone, it was like she had never existed.

"I had no idea," Holly continued.

"No worries at all—how could you?"

"Do you mind if I ask how it happened?"

"Tourists in a sports car they couldn't control rounded one of the corners too fast. They crossed the lane as my mom came around the corner and hit the truck she used to make her flower deliveries head-on."

"Oh my god. Again, I am so so sorry," Holly said. "If I wasn't being oh-so-careful on these roads, I'd reach over and give you a hug."

"Thanks." I have to admit that helped. Both the fact Holly was being careful and that she acknowledged a hug would be nice. There was something about her that made it easy to say things I had avoided talking about—and the big reason I'd stayed away for the ten years since it happened. Still, I tried to shrug it off a little. "It's been a long time now. I was in college. People have forgotten."

"But you haven't. And you shouldn't. I'm sure she was an amazing mother."

"She really was," I said. "You would have loved her. She was a gardener, too, and had a flower shop in Pacific Grove."

"Which flower shop?"

"Penny's Blooms."

"I love that shop! It's still there."

"Yeah, her friends kept it going. I have to admit I haven't been back to see it yet. She also planted a succulent garden at our home that is really wonderful."

"I'm sure it is. I would love to see it someday."

"That would be nice. Maybe you can show me how to take better care of it. I feel like it's not particularly happy at the moment."

"I would love that."

At that point, we had reached the first of our stops along the coast: Nepenthe. Known for offering a spectacular view from its restaurant overlooking the ocean, the compound also featured one of the coolest shops: The Phoenix. I dutifully checked it out while Holly went up to drop her wares off to the chef. Nepenthe was in the same general area as the ultra-luxurious Post Ranch Inn and Ventana, where Holly also made quick stops. They were lovely, but I think I preferred my little Hallmark movie lodge, although even at these swanky stops Holly knew

Chapter Six

everybody by name. In general, there seemed to be an amazing level of camaraderie among the denizens of Big Sur.

As Holly mentioned, our last stop was Esalen, the well-known education-and-retreat center. We turned down the steep grade that led into the property and Holly introduced herself to the person at the front gate. After a check of a clipboard, we got a nod and continued down. For me, Esalen was a blast from the past. I had forgotten just how beautiful the view was—with the property's gorgeous gardens and huge pine trees framing the ocean in the background. When I was growing up, my mom had loved coming to Esalen. A few times a year, she would help out friends who were running gardening workshops or painting workshops or these wacky dance workshops where everyone spun around in their own little happiness bubbles and bring me along. Never my dad. As by-the-book law enforcement dude, he was not a fan (as you might imagine), so it was me who was by her side as she danced around in ecstasy. Even as a child, I wondered how two such disparate people ever got together.

Holly parked near the kitchen area of the lodge. She told me she would be chatting with the chef for about half an hour to go over the next order, so I took the chance to walk through the property. I walked up a hill through the garden, which was filled with blooming yellow and red poppies along with the rows of lettuce, kale, carrots, and other vegetables, and then down the other side.

There I crossed a bridge that ran over a river that led to a spectacular waterfall and, in the distance, saw the two original houses that had been built by intrepid souls for a hot springs retreat a century earlier. I then passed a blue building that was labeled as the "Art Barn," where I was surprised to find Brody Montgomery sitting outside on the grass in a circle with a group of people fiddling with cameras. I tried to tiptoe by, but Brody looked up as I passed. He motioned to the group to keep doing whatever fiddling it was they were doing before waving to me to stop and walking up the bluff.

"Well, well, if it isn't the *Carmel Today* reporter."

"And the *National Geographic* photographer."

He laughed. "Yeah, sorry about that. Jen pushes my buttons a bit. She's my cousin and has been needling me since we were kids."

"Between Chelsea and Jen, you seem to be pretty connected."

"It's a smaller community out here than it would seem at first," he said. "Speaking of which, what are you doing here?"

"I'm exploring Big Sur today—you know, part of my job as a *Carmel Today* reporter—and Holly offered to bring me along on her stops. You?"

"They have this artist-in-residence thing here and this month that's me."

"That's cool."

"Yeah, I grew up not far from here so spent a lot of time at this place growing up."

"I actually did as well."

Chapter Six

"You went to the Gazebo school, too?"

"No, just came to workshops sometimes when my mom was assisting her friends."

"My mom was here all the time, too. I wonder if they knew each other."

"Hard to say. I can't ask mine. She died when I was in college."

"Oh, Sam, I'm so sorry."

"Thanks. I get that a lot."

"A lot of what?"

"People saying they are sorry for things—my mom dying, my dad getting Alzheimer's. Part of the reason I avoided coming home for so long, I guess."

"Well, then, I'm sorry for that, too."

"Again, thanks. I do appreciate it."

"But, if I may say: Selfishly, I'm happy you came back."

I smiled. Okay, so maybe Brody wasn't so bad, but I was still trying to put his Big Sur upbringing together with Jen's comment that his dad and Bob were best friends. Not to mention Chelsea (Chelsea!). So, intrepid reporter that I am, I asked him.

"So, how's a Gazebo kid's dad best friends with Bob Carpenter?"

Brody laughed. "That's a good question. Jack is actually my stepdad. He met my mom here at Esalen about 20 years ago while on a retreat after his divorce from wife number three. They hit it off, he sold everything he owned in San Francisco, and they've been living in a house in the hills above Nepenthe ever since."

I smiled. "Nice."

"Yeah, he went full-on hippie." Okay, so that made me laugh. "Somehow he and Bob still get along, though."

"Is that also how you know Chelsea?" I asked.

Brody rolled his eyes. "I suppose. She didn't grow up around here…"

"She didn't?"

"Oh, no, she's from the Central Valley—Modesto or Merced, one of those cities. But when Bob and Barb moved here full-time, she followed, and I've had to endure her at their events. Like last night's."

"Tonight's, too? Are you going to the reception at Perch Gallery?"

"Of course. It's my friend Zeke's show, so I will be there. Like I said, it's a pretty small world out here, especially for those of us in the arts."

"Arts, huh? Does that include reporters?"

He laughed. "That definitely includes those who create art with words, Sam."

I suppose that was nice, right? Maybe I was wrong about him being a *complete* asshole.

CHAPTER SEVEN

I walked back and met Holly at the lodge. We had a little time to kill, so she suggested we take a seat in one of the Adirondack chairs on the lawn. We looked out at the ocean and just took it all in. It was quite the beautiful view, and I had to admit that so far writing about the area wasn't quite as painful as I had envisioned.

Unfortunately, it wasn't long before we had to leave if Holly was going to get me back to the Wildflower Inn in time to change for the gallery event. Holly and I went back up to Highway 1, made a left out of the driveway, and headed back north. Now that we were driving north, I felt a little better. Mostly because I wasn't about to fall off the edge of a cliff—just maybe rub against some rock walls when those coming the other way freaked out about the drop-off and strayed into the middle of the lane. It also helped that, again, Holly took the turns like a champ.

Holly dropped me off at the inn and I made a quick change into an outfit that felt like it resembled "gallery chic"—okay, so I mostly just added a cool scarf I picked up at The Phoenix shop to my usual tank top/cotton sweater combo. Still, it was enough (I hoped) to avoid a look or a scolding about my attire from Mona or Stacy—or, worse, Chelsea—at the event. Soon I was driving back down Highway 1 on my own. Luckily, the Perch Gallery wasn't all that far from the inn. As I neared the location, I noticed a back-up of cars heading into the gallery's small driveway, so decided to continue on and found a space on the side of the road about a quarter-mile away. As I walked up to the gallery, I found a raft of valets greeting the backed-up cars. Made me glad I'd parked on the road. Not only was my car not anywhere near the same class as the fancy ones being parked, but it was much easier to walk than deal with the scrum at the valet stand.

As with the music venue opening, I was on the early side, so took the chance to walk around the grounds of the gallery complex, check things out, and take a few pictures. In addition to the gallery, which featured floor-to-ceiling windows, there was a café, an outdoor sculpture garden, and a grab-and-go style market that also featured knickknack style gifts. Cute place and a gorgeous location, but it sure felt smack in the middle of nowhere. Made me wonder how many

Chapter Seven

visitors they got looking for art on days when they weren't having a reception.

When I entered the art gallery, the reception was just getting underway. The gallery itself was quite stunning from the inside. The large windows brought the outdoor sculptures and surrounding trees into the mix with the art displayed inside. As the sun began to set, the lighting shifted on both the outdoor and indoor pieces, with little lights on the trees creating the illusion we were surrounded by stars. Just stunning.

It was an interesting mix of people that differed from the one the night before, at least so far—a lot of bohemian/outdoorsy-looking Big Sur types mixed in with the Carmel-by-the-Sea art crowd vs. the golf/wine crowd of the previous event. I backed into a corner so I could get some shots of the crowd surrounding the art and was just posting them on the sites when I heard a familiar voice behind me.

"Fancy meeting you here."

I turned to find Tom in the corner behind me, drink in hand and toupee on head. "Tom. Good to see you. I didn't know you were coming to this."

"I'm not here for long or in any official capacity. The gallery owner's a friend, so I said I would do a quick stop-by in support before meeting the general manager for dinner over at Post Ranch."

"Swanky."

"One of the perks of the business, Sam."

I laughed. "That's what the other writers kept telling me on the press trip in Maui."

Tom nodded. "It's important to enjoy the good parts of the job as they can help get you through the tougher days."

As if on cue, right at that moment Chelsea walked through the door in what I'm guessing was her version of "art gallery chic." It was actually a little (okay, a lot) over the top—her vibrant jacket looking more like something left over from a roadshow of "Joseph and the Amazing Technicolor Dreamcoat" than the art piece it was no doubt meant to resemble. Chelsea sashayed right past us and across the floor over to Barb and Bob, who I now saw were at the other end of the gallery talking to Mona and a gal I didn't recognize who had long red hair pulled back into a cool braid.

Not long after Chelsea arrived, Brody entered with more than a little panache. He was wearing a black t-shirt emblazoned with what looked to be an original line drawing of one of the sculptures I'd just seen outside etched in gray and a leather jacket. Even more impressive, he had on his arm a tall—like Mona's six-feet tall—and stunningly beautiful woman with long dark hair and light brown skin. I had a vague recollection of seeing her sitting with the group from his class but had no idea just how tall she was at the time.

Brody scanned the room, first looking in Chelsea's direction and then, when he saw Tom and me, making a beeline in our direction. In the corner of my eye, I could see Chelsea was not pleased with that turn of events.

Chapter Seven

"Sam. Good to see you. I want to introduce you to Sania. She's from Mumbai and has been doing a month-long work study at Esalen that includes taking my class. She mentioned she's interested in photojournalism, so I thought you might have some words of advice for her."

Tom gave me a quick nod as he backed away from us and out of the room.

"So nice to meet you, Sania," I said.

Before Sania could get a word out, Chelsea came clacking over in her platform shoes.

"Brody."

"Not now, Chelsea."

"Brody, you were supposed to call me."

"I'll get to it."

"When?" The desperation in her voice was so un-Chelsea-like it threw me a little.

Brody looked around as if seeking a distraction to get him away from the uncomfortable situation. He waved at a glowering guy with pasty white skin and spiky jet-black hair hiding in the corner on the other side of the gallery.

"Oh, look, it's Zeke. This is his art. Have you met Zeke yet, Sam?"

"I haven't and it would be great to get some quotes from him for the piece I'm writing." I gave Chelsea a look like *what the fuck?* But she didn't acknowledge my existence, her eyes boring into Brody's.

"I would be happy to introduce you," Brody said. "Sania, would you like to join us?"

"I'd love to."

Sania looked down on Chelsea, who maybe came up to her armpits, with what looked like pity in her eyes as the three of us made our way over to Zeke. Chelsea watched, rooted in her spot, trying her best to look like that's what she meant to do.

"Hey, Zeke, great show," Brody said. "I want to introduce you to Sania and Sam."

Zeke nodded while also looking like he wanted to disappear through the glass and away from the crowd. I totally got that impulse, so tried not to look too scary. I didn't want to spook him in the same way I hadn't wanted to spook that deer on the road on the way down.

"Really cool art," I said, hoping that sounded at least semi-intelligent. "Are the sculptures outside yours as well?"

"Some of them," he finally offered.

"I love how the windows bring them into the indoor space as well."

"Cool. That's what I was going for," Zeke said, brightening just a tad.

"I agree," said Sania. "The use of the illusory space really enhances the curvilinear shapes."

That's when Zeke's eyes really lit up. He looked like a stranger in a foreign land who finally found someone who speaks his language. "Yes!" Zeke said. "That was part of my iterative process."

"Nailed it, Zeke," said Brody.

The three of them kept chatting in their foreign "art" language, so after noting Zeke's quotes in my iPhone, I did a slow back away from their

Chapter Seven

conversation similar to the way Tom had ours earlier. I gave a small wave to Brody, who smiled and nodded as I walked over to find Mona.

"Where's the pup?" I asked when I found her, realizing how much I sounded like my dad at that moment.

"Little dogs and expensive sculptures don't mix," Mona said. "Besides, the drive into Big Sur tends to make him sick."

Mona looked at me and gave me a little side hug to silently acknowledge the sadness the words "drive into Big Sur" always caused us.

"How's the hotel?" Mona then asked, breaking the mood.

"It's really lovely," I said. "The new chef is amazing. Actually, they're all just so adorable."

"Sickening, isn't it?" she said, laughing.

"Totally."

"I have to make a few more rounds, but don't feel you have to stay too long here."

"Thanks. I think I got what I need. Be nice to enjoy that fireplace in my room."

"Go for it," Mona said, noticing Stacy waving from the bar on the other side. "And I'm back on stage."

"Thanks, Mona."

I did one final lap of the gallery before heading outside to start walking back to my car. When I passed the valet line, I found Chelsea already there waiting.

"Hey, Chelsea."

"Sam."

"Everything okay?"

"It's just fine, Sam."

"Okay, 'cuz it kind of seemed like something was going on in there…"

"None of your business, Sam."

"Okay…"

Just then a sporty and very bright red BMW was brought up. Chelsea handed the valet the ticket and a tip.

"This is your car? Nice!"

"Thanks," Chelsea said, brightening a little bit. "Aunt Barb and Uncle Bob got it for me for my birthday present."

"That's quite the birthday present."

"I know."

"And that's quite a bright red."

"Uh, Sam, it's vermillion."

"I stand corrected."

"It's okay, Sam. There are things you just aren't familiar with."

Was I really feeling sorry for her two minutes ago? I didn't take the bait. "That is probably very true, Chelsea."

Chelsea turns and touched my arm. "But that's not to say I don't appreciate you, Sam, just the way you are. I do."

I had to smile as I watched Chelsea leave in her bright red (sorry, vermillion) car, which I noticed had a vanity plate that said "CHLC." The weird thing is that instead of turning right to go back to Carmel, she turned left. Not sure if she was turned around or what, but the only thing in

Chapter Seven

that direction—unless she was going all the way down to Lucia or other points south—was Esalen and why would she be going down there?

Either way, it had been a long day, and I was ready to get back to my room at the Wildflower Inn. I walked back to my car, made the short drive back to the inn, and pulled into the space in front of my cabin. There, I lit the fireplace and popped open the bottle of local beer they had left for me along with a few small bites from the chef. I may have moaned with pleasure when I tasted the first one. His food was so good that I could definitely see people going out of their way to come to their restaurant.

Out of habit, I tried checking my phone. Nope, still no connection, and (I realized) no desire to hoof it over to the lodge to tap into the Wifi, especially since I had already posted the requisite photos of the art gallery reception. Instead, I crawled under the luscious down comforter and fell asleep to the sound of the river flowing behind the inn in the background. As I said, it had been a long day, but another great day. So far exploring Monterey was proving to be a lot more fun than I thought it would be.

CHAPTER EIGHT

The next day I got up, checked out, and said goodbye to Naomi and Evan and Kiwan. They were all there in the lodge when I left, offering big smiles and earnest pleas to come back that kept threatening to deteriorate my innate cynicism. I offered my own smiles and promises to return before heading back north up Highway 1 toward Carmel.

When I passed the area where I had seen the deer, I looked around to see if I could see any other creatures that might potentially dart in front of my car. Luckily, there weren't any. What I did see were some skid marks on the other side of the road near the area with the private property sign where I had pulled over the previous morning. I knew those marks weren't there the day before, so I looked to my left as I passed.

Chapter Eight

In my peripheral vision, I thought I glimpsed a splotch of red mixed in with the browns and greens and blues from the bluff and the coastline in the distance. That was weird. I made it maybe a quarter mile before my curiosity got the best of me. I made a u-turn and came back to the spot where I had parked while the deer meandered across the road. I got out of my car and looked down the embankment and there it was: Chelsea's car. Hard to miss the vermillion red and "CHLC" license plate.

I immediately checked my phone to see if I could call 911 but, nope, I was in one of the dead zones along the coast in this area. I scrambled down the embankment. When I got to the car, I noticed it was balancing somewhat precariously against a boulder that looked like it might give way at any moment, sending the car farther down the cliff to the beach below.

"Chelsea? Chelsea, are you in there?"

"Sam?" I heard a weak voice from within the car. "Sam, is that really you?"

"It's me, Chelsea. What the hell happened?"

"Get me out of here, Sam! Please! I'm afraid to move and I can't feel one of my legs."

From where I was standing, I could see in the window and noticed Chelsea was sitting as far as she could against the driver-side door to keep the car from tipping farther down the cliff. Not sure how much it helped with her lack of body weight.

"I tried to call 911 but had no signal," she continued weakly. I could tell she was really scared. Truth be told, so was I.

"I know. I tried from up on the road and got no signal either," I said. "I am going to try to get you out of there, okay?" I then thought for a moment as to just how it was I was going to manage that.

"Okay."

I assessed the situation as best I could and realized we could use her tiny size to our advantage.

"Chelsea, can you lower your car window?"

"Why the hell would I do that?"

"Because then I can grab your hand and pull you through, and we don't have to run the risk of the car continuing to move by opening the door."

Chelsea thought for a moment.

"Okay, I guess that's not a horrible idea."

"If you've got a better one, I'd love to hear it."

"I've been here all night and haven't come up with anything, so I suppose it will have to do."

Her snarky tone emerged even in—or due to?—this time of stress. I held off the urge to bail on her and call 911 down the road. Instead, I went up to my car and looked for something I could use to tie around my waist to keep me from flying down the hill with her in the event the car pulled us in that direction. I couldn't find anything in my car that resembled a rope so scrounged around alongside the fence. I found the rope tied between the two posts that previously held the private property sign. It was now on the ground at the top of the grade that Chelsea so obviously ignored

Chapter Eight

when she went off the side of the road. Ha. Sorry. I really didn't mean to make fun of the situation. While Chelsea's response to stress might be to up the snark, my response had always tended toward finding any possible humor in the situation. Something my superiors at the newspaper didn't particularly care for when I was covering crime scenes, I can tell you that.

I untied one side of the rope and made sure the other end was still tightly tied around the post before bringing it with me down the grade. When I got close to the car, I tied the rope around my waist and started inching my way down toward it.

"Okay, Chelsea. Push the button to lower your window."

"Okay." Her voice was weaker now. I heard her clicking on the button in the car, but the window wasn't budging. "It's not going down."

Shit, the battery must have run down.

"Okay, we'll have to try a different tack. Does the door open at all?"

"I think so. It's not locked. But I'm not opening the door, Sam. The motion will knock the car over." As if to emphasize her point, the car started rocking a little just with the motion she made in telling me that.

"Then we'll just have to do this very quickly. I'm going to be right next to the car so as soon as you open the door, grab my hand. Can you do that?"

"I don't know," she said very softly. I waited for a moment as I could feel the wind picking up and didn't want it disturbing the car anymore. "Okay, Sam. I can do this."

"Great. I'm going to count to three and then you open the door and grab my hand."

"On three or after three?"

"On three, Chelsea."

"There's no 'go,' then, just three."

If it's unclear to the editor, it's unclear to the reader. Her frequent refrain in the office started swirling in my head. Egads, she really couldn't help herself, could she?

"Yes, Chelsea, just three," I said, scooting as close to the car as I could get while still on firm ground. "Okay, ready?"

"No, wait, one second. I have to undo my seat belt."

"What the fuck are you doing with your seat belt still attached?"

"Don't yell at me, Sam!"

I took a breath. "I'm not yelling. Okay, are you ready?"

"Yes."

"Okay… One, two, THREE."

Chelsea opened the door, and I managed to grab her whole arm and pull her out of the car and onto the ground next to me. We both sat there for a moment, our hearts racing. The car didn't fall, thank god, but was teetering just a bit.

Once my heart stopped doing the meringue (the dance, not the dessert) in my chest, I asked Chelsea: "Can you walk at all?"

Chapter Eight

"I'm not sure. One leg seems fine, but I can't even feel the other one."

"Okay, let's start by scooching our way up the hill. When we get to a level place, we will try to stand you up, okay?"

"Okay."

Chelsea used her arms to push her way up the hill until we got to a place that was not far from the top and relatively level.

"Okay, now put your arm around my shoulder, and I'll help you stand. Which leg is the banged up one?"

"The right one."

I got on her right side and was, for the second time in two days, happy for the good six inches I had on her as I tried to pull her to her feet.

"Yeow," she cried out when she tried to stand. Her leg was obviously broken. It was sticking out at such an unnatural angle, I was trying not to look at it so it wouldn't make me sick. I also didn't want to hurt the leg any further.

"Don't put any weight on it."

"I'm trying not to, Sam. Don't yell at me."

"I'm not yelling at you, Chelsea."

"You are yelling, and this has been a really stressful situation."

"I get that, and I don't want to make things worse, so let me get something to brace your leg before we move any farther."

Instead of trying to walk her up, I untied the rope I still had wrapped around myself and ran up to the car. I found an old tennis racket in the trunk and a blanket. I brought both out and used the rope to lash the racket around Chelsea's leg and create a bit of a brace—silently thanking all the Girl Scouts training I'd had as a kid.

When I had her stabilized, she was able, with my help, to finish scooching to the level area at the top of the grade.

"I'm going to have to go for help at some point."

"Don't leave me, Sam."

"I'm going to have to if we want to get out of here. There's no cell reception, and I don't want to risk hurting your leg further by putting you in the car."

"Don't leave me, Sam."

"I won't go far. I promise."

Just then, we heard a creaking and groaning. We both turned and looked toward the ocean as her car started to roll and made its final descent toward the shore. With that, Chelsea passed out. Great. Now what?

I laid the blanket over a passed-out Chelsea as I ran up to the road and tried to flag down whatever passersby I might find at this time of the day. Luckily, it wasn't too long before I saw a UPS truck heading north from Big Sur. I waved manically in the center of the road and the driver pulled over and yelled out from his cab.

"You okay?"

"No—my friend rolled her car over the embankment. I got her out, but she's going to need an ambulance. Can you call one when you get into cell phone range?"

Chapter Eight

"I'll radio it in. Hold tight!"

I didn't have to wait long before I heard the sirens, and an ambulance came to get Chelsea. By then, she'd woken up and, of course, berated the EMTs the whole time about how they were going about their job. As they slid her in the ambulance, I waved, realizing I never asked her just how she ended up going over the side of the embankment. I figured I would check in with her later and, after giving my statement to the CHP officer at the scene, headed home.

To say the office was interesting when I got there later that afternoon would be an understatement. I walked in the door and was immediately bombarded with a sea of faces—Tom, Terry, Stacy, Ben, plus the other members of the sales and admin staff—and voices asking questions.

"How the hell did you find her?"

"Have you heard she broke her leg in multiple places?"

"I tell you—that's why I stopped driving around Big Sur at night. So scary."

"You know, sometimes they don't find cars that have gone over the side for months—if ever."

Gee, thanks, Tottering Terry, for that insight.

Mona walked over and put her hands up to stop the chattering. "I just talked to Barb," Mona said. "She and Bob are with Chelsea at the hospital. The doctors said her leg is broken in two places, and they'll have to do surgery to pin one of the spots—or something to that effect—so she will be staying there for a few more days. But she will be fine."

This seemed to momentarily quell everybody's concern—and curiosity. "We still have an issue to get out and another to prep," Mona continued. "So unless any of you have more questions, let's try to get that done, okay?" As they started to disperse, Mona turned to me. "Sam, can I see you in my office?"

"Of course."

I followed Mona into her office and sat across her desk. Cornwall, who was lying happily in his custom dog bed on the ground next to the desk, seemed to know I needed a little comfort and immediately came up and crawled into my lap.

"How are you doing?" Mona asked, sitting behind the desk.

"I'm fine," I said, stroking Cornwall's back.

"Really? You've been through a lot in the past few hours."

"Chelsea's been through a lot. I was just there to help out."

"Thank god you did. Any idea how the accident happened? I didn't want to pry when I called the Carpenters at the hospital."

"We didn't talk about it. But I did notice one thing that was strange."

"Yes?"

Chapter Eight

"When we left the art gallery the night before her accident, she turned left to go south instead of turning right to come straight home."

"Not so odd, I suppose—she has a lot of friends in the area."

"I suppose. She just didn't mention it before she left."

"Well, again, thank god you were there." Mona let that sink in before continuing. "As you may guess, this puts us in a bit of a bind in terms of getting the magazine out. I hope you won't mind if we ask you to do some of Chelsea's proofreading of the stories."

"Happy to help out."

"Great. Obviously, since you are an hourly employee, we can just expand the number of hours you work in the office this month. In the meantime, I'll put feelers out for other editorial help, and you can continue working on your regular story assignments."

"Sounds good to me."

"I know you have a couple days off before your next stop on the itinerary, so hopefully you can get some rest."

"I will. My next scheduled visit isn't until Monday in Monterey, although I am supposed to do a walk through downtown sometime this weekend. It's not a problem. I'll stroll around on Sunday afternoon to see if anything pops out as important to include."

"Perfect. We are still on for dinner tomorrow night, correct?"

"We are indeed. Uncle Henry is looking forward to it."

Mona smiled. "Good. It'll give us a chance to really chat without the possibility of prying ears, as it were."

I looked around the closed doors to the office and wondered who or what she might be referring to but said nothing.

"I look forward to that."

I left Mona's office and went back to my desk. I found Tom at his usual spot, poring over the copy layouts on his screen.

"Hi Tom. Mona asked me to help you out with any proofreading since Chelsea will be laid up for a while."

"Thanks. I appreciate that. Luckily, the issue that's shipping to the printer on Monday has already been proofread, but when the final proof comes back from the printer later next week, it would be great to have another pair of eyes on it."

"Happy to. Hey, I'm curious about something I heard when I was out and about the past few days."

"Shoot."

"Someone said that the old editor, Buddy Wheeler, used to cycle through Chelsea types all the time."

"Well, they weren't all *Chelsea*."

We both laughed. "Yes, I can see she's definitely one of a kind."

"But, yeah, Buddy's MO was to get kids right out of college because they were cheap and would do exactly what he told them to do. After maybe a year or so, he'd be an ass about something, and they would realize he was making promises about promotions and raises he couldn't keep, and they'd leave."

"Do you mind if I ask why you've stayed so long, Tom?"

Chapter Eight

Tom sat back and thought a moment. "I don't know—habit?" he said, laughing. "The truth is, I really enjoy the work. It's what I've done my whole life. I love the Monterey Peninsula and telling the stories of the people who live here. And while print magazines may be a dying art, I still love the process. Each issue, it's like we go through a whole cycle of life, you know? From idea through research and writing through art and production and then to a finished copy. It's a great sense of accomplishment. Not to mention the perks that come with it. Like I mentioned last night at the gallery, events like that where you discover new artists or get the first chance to taste the food from a new chef..."

"How was last night's meal at Post Ranch, by the way?"

"Amazing," Tom said, "And the one at Wildflower Inn?"

"Pretty amazing as well."

"See? That kind of special treatment can be addictive. There's also attending industry conferences or press trips like your one to Maui. I'll admit it's also nice having people know who you are around town. Being connected, you know? So, yeah, Buddy could be derisive, but he was manageable. At least he was with me. I think he knew not to push too hard, or he'd have to put out the magazine himself, and he definitely didn't want to do that." Tom laughed again.

"And then he just disappeared?"

"Oh, he didn't disappear. He resigned. He knew the old owner was starting to think of selling. Hugh Tompkins was getting really old. I think he was over 90. Buddy was getting older, too, and starting to complain about our constantly cool weather. On a press trip to the Palm Springs area, Buddy stayed at a resort that had some townhomes for sale. He fell in love with the place and bought one. When he presented the idea of a retirement buyout, Hugh jumped at it."

Tom sat back and thought a moment. "The only thing that was a little odd was how sudden it was. Buddy came in after hours one day, wrote his resignation letter directly into the issue about to go to press, packed his things, and left. I mean, while it actually wasn't completely out of character for someone so self-obsessed to not care how he left things when he did, it was a bit of a surprise."

"Wait, he wrote his resignation letter into the magazine?"

Tom laughed. "Yeah, he used his monthly editor's letter to essentially say 'see ya suckers.'"

"Do we still have that issue? I'd love to see it."

"We should still have the issue back in the archives. In a way, it was a typical Buddy move to do it so publicly. Figured everyone in the world—our little world here in Carmel, at least—needed to know. Then he flew the coop, as it were. The truth is, by then he'd burned quite a few bridges, and Carmel wasn't the welcoming home it had been for him for all those years. The letter was both a farewell to the friends he still had and a thumbing of his nose to those he'd burned."

Chapter Eight

"Wow. So interesting. Thanks, Tom. As a newbie, I appreciate having the back story."

"Happy to help. As you know, I love this magazine. I was really happy when Mona was brought on board—she's a real class act—and that you were brought on and that we can all continue to do what we love here."

That was sweet. It reminded me of what my old tennis coach, Mr. Tanaka (sorry, the "Steve" wasn't sticking), had said. Aren't we all just looking for something we love as much as they do?

I was still a little curious, though, about Buddy's departure, so before leaving, I tried to find the issue with the resignation letter. I started at my computer and looked at the issues archived online, but as part of the website redesign after the new owners took over, only those from the new regime (as it were) were included. I went into the back storeroom, where they stored decades of old issues in a huge wall of cubby holes filled with binders—the archives, as Tom called them. One copy of each issue was placed in a binder that represented a whole year's worth of magazines. The binders went back decades. I found the binder from the year when Buddy left—it had been a little over 14 months, but the timing made it two binders ago. I flipped through and found just 11 issues in the binder. None of them had Buddy's editor's letter that I could see. They jumped from an editor's letter where Buddy talked about his excitement over the opening of a new restaurant in town, among other stories in the magazine, to one from Tom on his new role as interim editor while the magazine went through its transition to new ownership. Huh. Interesting.

As I was looking through the binders, Tottering Terry came walking in.

"Hey, Terry. How's it going?"

"It's going, Sam. It's going. Just getting a few more copies of last month's issue. Carl, Bill, and George were chuffed that I mentioned our weekly poker game, so I thought I would bring them each a copy."

"That's nice. Hey, Terry, do you know anything about the issue where Buddy used his editor's letter to announce his resignation?"

"Do I ever. That puppy caused more than a little drama around here."

"In what way?"

"Just how sudden it was. No one knew until they were doing the final proof of the magazine."

"Crazy."

"Crazy is right, sister. Why are you asking?"

"Curious. People kept mentioning him, so I wanted to see exactly what he said."

"Isn't it in the binder?"

"It's not. Every issue from that year except that one seems to be here."

"Huh. Well, as you can see, I tend to snatch a few extra issues to keep in my own personal files at home. Want me to bring you a copy?"

"That would be great. Thanks," I said, even though I would have preferred not to wait for the next time I saw Terry. Sometimes our paths

Chapter Eight

didn't cross for weeks, so after leaving the storeroom, I walked by Mona's office to see if she had a copy of the magazine. The door was closed, and I could hear her talking on the phone inside. I decided to send her a text asking about the missing issue later.

Instead, I went back to my desk and tapped into the computer database to see if I could find out where Buddy lived. My dad's comment about his disappearance being weird kept ringing in my ear and nothing I had heard from the others had quelled my curiosity. Maybe a little walk or drive by his old house would help. Unfortunately, the only thing listed was his post office box. Because so many of the houses in Carmel-by-the-Sea still have quaint (but not at all practical) names like "west side of Dolores three houses north of 4th Avenue" or "Rose Cottage," most residents used their P.O. Box as their address. Obviously, a little more digging was in order. Someone had to know where he lived, right?

CHAPTER NINE

Between Lizzy's constant cajoling and running into Mr. Tanaka, on Saturday morning I was back out on a tennis court for the first time in years. I cobbled together an outfit from clothes I used to wear to run along the Venice Beach boardwalk every morning and made my way out to the closest courts, which were at Mission Ranch. Lizzy somehow finagled us a reserved court even though she wasn't a member or a guest of the hotel—not sure if it was tennis related (she knew every coach in town) or dog related (similar connections). Lizzy brought me a racket since I'd used my old one as a splint on Chelsea's leg and—can you believe it—she hadn't returned it. (More inappropriate humor, I realize.)

"Don't worry. We'll just have a light hit," Lizzy said before immediately sending one of her

Chapter Nine

gazillion-mile-an-hour shots my way and then laughing hysterically.

"Funny, Lizzy. Funny," I said. "It's been 20 years since I've even picked up a racket."

"I know, I know. Sorry."

Lizzy sent a nice loping shot my way and I did my best to hit it back. After a while, my rhythm came back, and we were having some nice rallies. Then the rallies got a little more competitive, with each of us trying to run the other back and forth from doubles alley to doubles alley. Of course, every time Lizzy wanted to end the point, she would either give me a drop shot or one of her patented topspin lobs that hit the fence before I could get a racket on it. I might have offered a few choice words every time that happened. She just grinned. After a good hour of hitting and some yelling, we started walking back to our cars.

"That was fun," Lizzy said.

"I suppose."

"Come on, Sam. You enjoyed yourself. Better than just walking Buster every day."

"Okay, fine. It was fun. You haven't lost any of your strokes, Lizzy."

"Oh, I've lost a ton. I am nowhere near competitive shape."

"Well, you don't really have to be in competitive shape these days, so that makes sense."

"I suppose."

"Did I tell you I ran into Mr. Tanaka out at Carmel Valley Golf Lodge?"

"No. That's so fun!"

"He told me he offered you a job teaching tennis out there."

"His wasn't the only offer. Every resort in town offered me a job," she said, nodding back at Mission Ranch. "Having WTA Tour credentials made me very popular."

"Why didn't you take any of them up on it?"

"I don't know. The truth is I couldn't think of anything more depressing than having my whole life being centered around hitting a little yellow ball."

"But you love the game."

"I do love it, but I love a lot of other things as well. I spent 10 years—heck, my whole life up until recently—focused on that one thing and one thing only."

"At least you got to travel to some amazing places on the tour."

"Absolutely. I loved that playing gave me the opportunity to travel, but even then I'd only get a few hours here and there to actually see the town we were visiting. Most of it was another hotel room, another tennis court, another locker room, then back to the hotel, and then get on another plane and repeat."

"I get it."

"Every once in awhile in those towns, a bunch of us would play hooky and find a spot—a cool restaurant or watering hole. We'd meet actual locals versus the same umpires, coaches, and tournament officials we saw at every single stop. And that, that was fun. Truth be told, except for

Chapter Nine

winning—which, as you well know, I absolutely love more than anything—it was the most fun I had while on the tour. I promised myself that's what I would do when I left."

"Makes sense."

"I have to say, in a way, it's made me love tennis even more. I get to kind of miss it now. So, when the high school coach offered me the part-time after-school gig, I took it."

"Mr. Tanaka said you're bringing the team over to the resort once or twice a month."

"Yeah, with two of us plus the coach, we can really do some good work with them. I think Tanaka likes working with the public park kids again. That swank club gave him all the resources he's ever wanted, but it's also a lot of setting up cocktail hour round robins. The joy in the faces of the kids reminds him why he loves tennis. Heck, it reminds me why I love tennis."

"I feel like that's been a running theme for me this week."

"Tennis?"

"People who love what they do." I told her about meeting Jen and Holly, and Naomi and Ethan and Kiwan, before all the drama happened with Chelsea, whose accident naturally everyone had already heard about.

"Maybe that's the theme of your Monterey story."

"Maybe it is—speaking of which, I've gotta run. This is my only free day this weekend, so I have to pick up Buster before visiting my dad and then am meeting Mona and Uncle Henry for dinner."

"Sounds fun."

"You're welcome to join us."

"I would, but Dominic was scheduled to help me at the café tonight and he isn't feeling well. I have to head back and relieve Diego."

"Diego is there?"

"Yeah, it's his day off, but he said he would fill in for a couple hours while we played tennis."

"That was nice of him."

"He's a nice guy. As you well know," Lizzy said, giving me a look. So, yeah, I may have failed to mention I once had a fling with Lizzy's older brother, Diego. Part of a series of instances where I acted out in the first few years after my mom's death.

"Yes, I know."

After a pause, Lizzy said, "He's seeing someone," as if she wasn't sure how I would take it.

"He is? Good." And I meant it. Good for him.

"I wasn't sure if I should tell you."

"Why not? That was a one-time thing after my dad's retirement party, Lizzy."

"A one-time thing after a lifetime of ogling each other. Then you ran back to L.A. and, well, now you're back."

There was that.

"Really. There's nothing there." I fiddled with my bracelet again and thought of Roger. I had to admit that its use as a talisman wasn't helping me as much as it was before. I wasn't blind to the fact

Chapter Nine

that most long-distance relationships—or even potential relationships—don't make it, especially ones with 2,000 miles of ocean in between them.

Still, I didn't really see anything with Diego, either. While he was adorable and super sweet and we'd had an ongoing crush on each other growing up, the only thing our tryst had done was make me realize how little we actually knew each other outside of our families.

"Really, Lizzy. Nothing," I reiterated.

"Okay. Good to hear. Diego and Marisol actually work well together. She's an investigator with the Monterey district attorney's office."

"Oh my god, more law enforcement types."

Lizzy peered over her sunglasses to give me another look. "Indeed, although you should talk. What's the deal with Mr. Maui Detective?"

I looked at my watch. "Oops, look at the time. Now I've really got to go."

"You're deflecting."

"Am I?" I said, starting to back away. "We'll do this again soon."

"Promise?"

"Scout's honor."

I swung home, took a quick shower, picked up Buster, and made the walk over to my dad's assisted living facility. As usual, as Buster and I entered the lobby, we paused to let the little old ladies (and they were mostly all ladies) sitting by the door "ooh" and "aah" over him. They would bring out their silly "baby/puppy talk" voices as they reached out to pet him and told stories about their own long-gone but still beloved pets. Carmel's reputation as one of the dog-friendliest cities in the country meant they had all had at least one.

Buster was used to the attention. He ate it up, wagging his big ole brindle-colored butt back and forth in happiness as they pet him. Then, when I passed the locked door that let me into the memory care part of the center (no Alejandra today—must be her day off) and finally reached my dad, his face brightened at Buster's presence.

"Buster!"

"Yep, Dad. Buster's here to say hi."

Buster did his usual twirl three times before sitting right on my dad's foot. They both sat contentedly with big grins that were, in a word, adorable.

Then my dad turned back to me, did his usual squint, and started in with the usual. "Working a case?"

"Kind of." In response to his furrowed brows, I continued. "Well, to start, I helped rescue a colleague from a cliff off Highway 1 in Big Sur."

"Big Sur. That's where your mom…"

"I know, Dad. I know. This one wasn't in the same place and didn't involve another driver that I could see, but I found her car dangling off the side of the road."

"That's strange."

"Really strange. She's someone I work with at *Carmel Today*."

"*Carmel Today*."

"Remember? That's where I work now."

Chapter Nine

"Right. With Mona."

"Right."

My dad closed his eyes and thought for a moment. "He had a cat, you know."

"Who had a cat?"

"The guy. The guy we were talking about. The guy before Mona."

"Buddy Wheeler?"

"Buddy? Buddy. Yeah. I think that's it."

"Sure it was a cat, Dad? Everyone here has dogs. Like Buster here."

"Buster!"

With that, the dinner plates started coming out and his focus shifted. I knew I'd lost my chance to get any more out of him, so I made my exit and headed back to the house. Mona was already there when I got home, throwing ingredients into a salad bowl and drinking a glass of wine while Henry was cooking outside on the grill. Cornwall was sleeping away on the dog bed next to the dining room table, so I let Buster off his leash. Buster and Cornwall did their doggy butt sniff and then both circled three times and slumped next to each other on the dog bed.

I joined Mona in the kitchen, and she pointed to a copy of the magazine sitting on the counter. "That's the issue you're looking for."

"You did have it!" I said. "Great. So weird they didn't have it in the archives."

"Barb sent it to me back when they were first offering me the job, probably because it had Buddy's resignation letter in it."

"Makes sense."

"You can see how thin the issue is. That was part of their pitch—that I could help grow the magazine back to what it had been in years past."

"Which is something you're already doing."

"I'm trying, anyway. It hasn't been easy."

I went over to the dining room table and sat down. I flipped to the editor's letter in the magazine and read it as Mona continued tossing the salad. "His resignation-slash-editor's letter seems pretty straightforward," I said.

"For a guy racing out of town, yeah."

"Still, there's something a little off about it."

"In what way?"

"I can't put my finger on it, really. Do you mind if I keep the magazine for a little bit?"

"Be my guest. I don't need it for anything."

Mona brought the salad bowl over to the dining room table adjacent to the kitchen. I poured myself a glass of wine while Uncle Henry finished cooking the fish on the grill just outside the door.

"So, what was the story with Buddy?" I asked.

"What about him?"

"As you mentioned, he seemed to have raced out of town. Dad said he thought it was odd, so I was curious."

"You know, I was gone the years he was in charge of the magazine, so I never really knew the man. As you can see in the letter, he said he was hellbent on retiring to Palm Springs. Tired of the cool weather, I guess."

Chapter Nine

"I guess."

"From what I understand, he also burned a lot of bridges in his last few years."

"That's what Tom said."

"Tom would know. He is the institutional memory at that place. Along with Stacy, although she hasn't been there quite as long as Tom has."

"Oh, and Dad said he had a cat."

"You know, that's right. I think he did," said Henry, coming into the kitchen/dining area with a sizzling platter. "I forgot about that. One of those big 20-pound Maine Coon- or Norwegian Forest-type cats. Buddy would even put pictures of it in the magazine. That cat was quite the character, as I recall, and would stroll around the neighborhood greeting people."

"Which neighborhood? Do you know where he lived?"

"I think it was a few blocks north of Ocean around Lincoln or Monte Verde," Henry said. "One of those bungalows nestled into the canyon there."

"Buddy really sounds like an odd duck," I said.

"You don't know the half of it," said Mona. "I didn't want to bring this up in the office. There's something about the place that, even in a closed office, I feel like there are prying eyes and ears everywhere. The truth is Buddy caused a lot of trouble."

"What kind of trouble?"

"From what I understand, he would occasionally borrow from the magazine's coffers to pay off personal debts he'd accrued."

"What debts?"

"Nothing nefarious—that I knew of, anyway. He would just dip in here and there to cover some outlandish expense."

"Which is illegal, I would like to point out," Henry offered.

"Very," I said. "Do you know why no one called him on it?"

"Pride, I suppose," Henry said.

"Whose pride?"

"Hugh Tompkins, the old owner. Hugh has always been a very secretive guy, especially when it came to his finances, so I'm sure he didn't want it getting out that someone was embezzling from him."

"What kind of outlandish expenses was Buddy making?"

"According to Barb," Mona said, "they mostly came from Buddy trying to act like some of the people he featured in the magazine who had expensive tastes. That can be one of the pitfalls of working for a magazine in the luxury lifestyle market, Sam."

"Not an issue when I was covering crime in L.A.," I said, laughing.

"Quite the opposite. In this industry, you see up close some of the trappings of wealth and prestige. You just have to always keep in mind that we're just covering them, not living their lives."

Chapter Nine

"How have you managed to avoid those pitfalls?"

"Your mother, for one."

"In what way?"

"Well, she was my role model growing up. Even though she started as my babysitter, she was only about ten years older than I was. The truth is, starting in grade school, I spent more time with her than I did with my own mom, who was always off on some lark and leaving me in your mom's teenage hands every afternoon after school. She was the happiest person I knew, even when she was young."

"She always had a smile on her face," Henry offered, with a smile of his own.

"And could talk to anybody," said Mona.

"That's how I feel about you, Mona," I said. "You seem so comfortable no matter who you are talking to or whatever environment you're in."

"I suppose I learned that from her."

"Yet you still went to New York and worked for *Vogue*. That's *so* not Mom."

"I'm not saying we wanted the same things in everything in life. Penny had her flowers and trees. She was able to find beauty everywhere. Living in this area made her very happy. I was drawn to fashion and travel. Carmel felt small to me. I wanted some adventure and to find a bit of the beauty out in the world. Kind of like you did, my dear," Mona said, looking at me.

"Although in my case it was less beauty..." I said.

"Than investigating mysteries—criminal and otherwise," Henry offered. "Not surprising considering that's all your dad and I talked about when you were growing up."

"What was similar to you, Sam, was that when I left, I couldn't wait to get out of here and hit the big city…" said Mona.

I looked at Mona as she was speaking. Still so elegant. I remembered how glamorous she always looked to me when she would sweep in for a visit like a benign Cruella de Ville (no puppy coats but always incredibly stylish) and tell us the latest stories about fashion week in Paris or club hopping in New York.

Then I noticed her exchange a quick glance with Henry. Although to me, Uncle Henry was OLD—with his professorial tweed jackets, black-rimmed glasses, and constantly bemused expression—he was the type of person who probably looked the same age in his 20s as he did now at almost 70, except for the fact his hair was getting more salt than pepper by the day. Henry was quite a few years younger than my dad and now that I thought about it, he was probably only a few years older than Mona, which made me wonder how much time the two of them spent together or if they even knew each other when they were growing up.

"…and, I have to say, New York was wonderful," continued Mona, sounding a bit wistful. "When you're young, it really is the most magical and exciting city in the world. The opposite

Chapter Nine

of sleepy, quirky, artsy Carmel. I would return home for the holidays all full of myself wearing clothes from the *Vogue* closet and thought I was pretty darn spectacular."

"You were pretty darn spectacular," I said, voicing what I had just been thinking.

She touched my arm. "You're sweet. I did look fabulous, of course, but I could tell it didn't impress your mom."

"You always made an impressive entrance, Mona," Henry said and got a smile from her. "But those weren't the kinds of things that impressed Penny."

"Exactly, Henry," said Mona. "It's not that she wasn't happy for me or proud. She was. It just wasn't her thing. I mean, she had her little flower shop and her hippy-dippy friends, which to me at the time were so small town."

Mona shrugged. "It didn't mean we didn't care about each other. She was the cool older sister I never had. And when she married your dad, they all—and that includes Henry here, of course—treated me like I was still part of the family."

Henry nodded his approval. "You were."

Mona thought for a moment. "Looking back, you know what I remember? Just how happy she always was. Like I said, the happiest person I knew."

"That she was," Henry said. "Without exception."

It was nice to be talking about my mom. It's like I could feel the warmth of her presence returning to the house—a house that had felt so empty for so long.

"So, what made you come back?" I asked.

"I don't know," Mona said, making an almost imperceptible look in Henry's direction. "I had made my way to New York and into the pages I'd grown up reading. I conquered the big city—the biggest city, really—and it was exciting and wonderful. After a while, though, I realized that while the pretty clothes were fun, ultimately, they were just things."

"Trappings of success," said Henry.

Mona nodded. "Trappings is right. The other thing I learned the more I rose in the ranks and spent time with all those fancy people is that a lot of the rich and famous that others admire and aspire to be are not actually all that happy."

Henry put a hand over hers. Now I was dying to ask what the heckety-heck was going on between them or had gone on between them or might go on between them but figured it would be easier to ask them each separately and not disrupt Mona's train of thought.

"I still loved my job, but after a while, I started to think about returning home," said Mona. "I just wish I had done it before your mom died."

Hearing that and looking at the two of them, I realized it was the first time Henry and I had invited anyone over to the house since I had returned home. Any socializing we did was over

Chapter Nine

at Lizzy's cafe. Perhaps because my mom was the one who loved bringing groups of people together, it just hadn't occurred to us to do it, and made me realize again just now quiet the house had become.

My reverie was broken as Mona continued: "Of course, bringing it back to Buddy, it seemed that he was never going to leave or would have allowed Hugh to hire me on. There aren't that many lifestyle magazines on the peninsula that aren't either family-run or in some other way inaccessible to outsiders—say run by real estate companies or editorial in name only."

"And with the way print has been going in the last decade…"

"Oh, Henry, don't depress me further."

Henry smiled that wry smile of his and I realized I was still confused about something: "Wait, how did you find out Buddy was in debt?"

"It came out in the audit that Bob and Barb had their CPA conduct before the final sale went through."

"Oh, wow."

"Oh, wow is right. They actually used the audit to negotiate a cheaper price. I think by that point Hugh was just happy to rid himself of any potential lawsuits from advertisers, so he agreed and had them sign all sorts of legal papers saying as much. Of course, they didn't tell me any of this when they offered me the job. I found out later."

"Wow again."

"You said it. Between that and the dysfunction I found among the staff, I'm going to be honest and say that I might not have taken the job if I'd known."

"Speaking of dysfunctional staff, have you talked to Chelsea yet?" I asked

Mona actually laughed out loud before resuming her usually noncommittal smile. "I did. She was very groggy."

"Does she have any idea how her car went off the road?"

"None. She got really weird when I asked about it and said she didn't want to talk about it. She did want to make sure you were keeping to the itinerary she created for you."

"Of course, she did."

CHAPTER TEN

The next day, after walking up to town from the house, I sat in a courtyard in downtown Carmel-by-the-Sea looking through the local visitors guides and magazines I picked up from the kiosk outside the library on Lincoln and Ocean. I did not pick up *Carmel Today*, although it was kind of fun to see it there. Part of me wanted to open it up to my Maui story and say to people walking by, "Hey, I wrote this, you know!"

Flipping through the visitors guide put together by the local chamber of commerce, it was kind of funny how many places I didn't recognize. There were also all sorts of "fun facts" they included that I will admit I didn't know: 50 restaurants within a square mile! Downtown has 41 secret passageways and courtyards! A city ordinance bans high heels!

Really? I thought. *Should someone tell Stiletto Stacy?*

I started to see the value in visiting your own city as a tourist—especially if it's a city you have been away from for a dozen years. Obviously, there were way too many things to include in my story—a hundred galleries and dozens of tasting rooms and even more shops and cute-as-a-button hotels to go with the aforementioned 50 restaurants—so I tried to figure out how I might frame the town and its relationship to the greater region to someone who hadn't been here before or, like me, was discovering it all over again.

One of the themes I noticed and started playing with was the number of intrepid women who seemed to have played a strong role. An odd thing to call out, perhaps, in a story "on the road" to a men's golf tournament, but it stood out. Not just in the people I had met this week—Barb, Jen, Holly, Naomi—but in the history of Carmel-by-the-Sea itself. For instance, I learned La Playa Carmel was first turned into a hotel in the early 1900s by a woman named Agnes "Alice" Signor. Then there was Cypress Inn, best known because the actress Doris Day was a co-owner starting in the 1980s and insisted that dogs be as welcome as the humans. Lesser known was the fact that it was the site of the city's first art gallery and in the early 1900s used by a woman artist named Mary DeNeale Morgan. A lot of the artists who ended up in Carmel in the early 1900s seemed to have been women—many of them single women.

Chapter Ten

As a somewhat intrepid (I would like to think anyway) single woman, I kind of liked the idea of these role models. With that thought in mind, I started walking around to see what else I could find, other than all the people and dogs and dogs and people walking along with me. As I meandered through the streets, I started peeking in cute stores (including a cannabis dispensary that definitely was not there when I was growing up), restaurants, cafes, chocolate and candy shops, and wine-tasting rooms. Unlike those in the Carmel Valley, these wine tasting rooms were a little smaller, with some attached to art galleries.

As I passed one of them, I looked inside and was surprised to see one of the intrepid women I had met recently: Jen, the R.O.C. winemaker. She was in one of the tasting rooms (not for her winery, which was odd) pouring samples from a bottle of wine into four glasses for a group of giggling gals. I walked around the corner and into the tasting room.

"Hey there, Jen—what are you doing here?"

"Hi, Sam! Good to see you! I was in town dropping off cases of our wine to one of the shops," said Jen. "My friend Donna texted that she's caught in the traffic coming in from Monterey and had these clients stopping by her wine-tasting room. I said I would help out until she gets here."

"That's so nice of you."

"Oh, we do this kind of thing all the time for each other. There is a group text for some of the boutique wineries in the area since we all wear a lot of hats and are often in different places throughout the county."

"Very cool. Do you need any help?" I asked.

"I got it covered. Want some?" she asked, holding up the bottle in her hand.

I looked at my watch. It was a little after 3 p.m. on a Sunday afternoon. I wasn't really expected to be anywhere, and I had walked into town.

"What the heck. Sure."

I took a seat at the counter, which gave me a great vantage point to watch the people walking along Ocean Avenue while also listening to the conversations at the tables around me—always a fun hobby of mine and good fodder, you know, for the story.

"This is a dry rosé that Donna makes. She crafts it entirely from free-run juice with no pressed grapes, which allows for its lovely aromas and pale pink hue. Donna uses mostly cool-climate pinot grapes indicative of Monterey's coastal terroir and ferments it at cold temperatures in stainless steel tanks, with no malolactic fermentation, which gives it a refreshing acidity and crisp finish."

I tried not to laugh at the description Jen gave with no hint of irony as I took a sip. It was very light and dry, which I liked. "Uh, nice," I managed with a smile.

"Glad you like it," Jen said, before noticing the table with the giggling gals was gesturing for their next round. "Be right back."

Chapter Ten

Just then my phone rang, and the notification said it was from Roger Kai, the Maui detective I'd gotten to know on my recent trip. Perfect timing, as I felt the warmth from the wine blend with the warmth I felt seeing his name on my phone.

"Hey Sam, how's it going?" Roger said. I could feel my heart beat just a little faster and was glad to know that the feelings I thought might be waning could still be conjured from his voice.

"You'll never believe where I am," I said as I answered.

"With you, I'd believe anything."

"I'm wine tasting."

"Very nice. A little early for that here in Hawaii, but I'm sure it's all work-related."

"You know, it totally is!"

I told him about my assignment to cover the region and all that had happened—including rescuing Chelsea from the edge of the cliff and the mysterious disappearance of the former editor-in-chief.

"Did anyone ever report him missing?" Roger asked.

"I don't think so. I mean, I guess he's not technically missing. He supposedly wrote a resignation letter that was printed in the magazine and then left for Palm Springs."

"Any forwarding address?"

I hadn't thought of that. If he was moving, why was his P.O. Box still listed as his address in the magazine's database? "No. All I found in our records was his local post office box. Maybe I should check with the folks over there."

"It also wouldn't hurt to talk to the local police department, just in case someone did report him missing."

"Good idea."

"I've been known to have them."

"What are you working on? A case?"

"Yeah, but not particularly exciting. Some smash-and-grabs at a couple jewelry stores in Lahaina."

"I'm sure you'll figure out who's behind it."

"Already have. We just can't tie them to it yet. I'm staking out their place now. Trash pick-up is early tomorrow morning in this area, so at some point today one of them should be bringing the bins out to the public space that is the street. I'm hoping we can find something in there with some DNA."

"Smart guy."

"You know it."

"If, you know, a bit…"

"Trash-obsessed?"

We both laughed. There was a pause.

"I miss you," he said. Damn, there go the butterflies again.

"I miss you, too. Wish you were here with me sipping this lovely rosé."

"Me, too."

"Maybe we can set something up."

Chapter Ten

"I'd like that. There's a forensics convention in San Francisco coming up in a couple months. That's near you, right?"

"Totally near me."

"I'll see if we can make that happen. Or, you know, my sister works for Hawaiian Airlines. Maybe I can use her benefits to hop on a flight for a long weekend one of these days."

Kaplump. That was my heart, but I was cool. "I'd like that."

"Me, too." Pause. "In the meantime, let me know what you learn about both Chelsea and that editor-in-chief."

"Will do."

"Bye, Sam."

"Bye." Between the wine and the sound of his voice, I enjoyed the buzz I was feeling, while also contemplating whether a relationship was ever going to be possible. Heck, maybe a long-distance thing was just what I needed after just coming out of such a dysfunctional one back in Los Angeles. Long-distance included the perks of knowing someone was thinking of me with the distance to figure out who the hell I was as an individual, especially now that I was back home. Maybe that was the wine talking. Before it could add any more to the conversation going on in my head, I spotted Lizzy walking quickly outside on the sidewalk. I tapped the window and she looked back in surprise and walked around the corner to come into the wine-tasting room.

"Sam, what are you doing here?"

"Research!" I said, holding up my wine glass.

"Of course, it is," Lizzy said, laughing.

Jen came over.

"How's it going over here?"

"Great," I said. "Jen, this is my friend Lizzy. She runs the Paws Up. Lizzy, this is Jen; she is the winemaker at R.O.C., the Carpenter's winery."

"Cool," they both said in unison.

"I love the Paws Up," Jen said. "Bring my dogs there all the time."

"And I love your wine," Lizzy said, "especially the viognier. I often recommend it to people at the café."

"Funny—that's the same wine Sam chose the other night at our event."

"You remembered that?" I asked.

"When it comes to wine, I remember everything," Jen said.

I left Lizzy and Jen gabbing away like old friends and walked over to the police department. It was just a few blocks out of the center of town and up a hill from where I had been sitting. There was a bit of déjà vu as I walked into a building I had visited many many times when my dad was the police chief.

There was a guy behind the plexiglass partition at the entrance that I didn't recognize. A newbie, judging from his age and the press of his uniform. His name tag read "Officer Hancock."

"Hello, officer," I said.

"What can I do for you, ma'am?"

"Ma'am? Ma'am? How old do you think I am?"

Chapter Ten

"It's a sign of respect, ma-..." He stopped mid-ma'am, so was smarter than he looked.

"Depends on the viewpoint, I suppose."

"What can I do for you?"

"Well, Officer Hancock, a couple things. The first is I'm wondering if you've heard anything about the investigation of the accident that happened down between Carmel Highlands and Big Sur a couple days ago."

"Not our jurisdiction. We pretty much stop at the city limits."

"I realize that's the county sheriff's territory. Just curious if you, you know, heard anything. I know word tends to get around in the law enforcement circles."

He looked at me curiously. "Hard to say, mah..."

"I'm going to make it easy on you, officer. You can call me Sam."

"Thank you, Sam." He smiled.

"I take it you are new."

"My first week. Can you tell?"

"No, not at all," I lied. "I'm just pretty familiar with the place. My dad was the police chief a while back."

"You're Chief Powers' daughter?"

"That I am."

"We heard about you."

"All good things, I hope."

He smiled an enigmatic smile that could mean so many different things. "Very good."

"Glad to hear. So ... what's the scoop on the accident?"

"Truthfully, I haven't heard anything. I do know they were able to recover the car yesterday."

"Interesting." I made a mental note to check in with Lizzy's brother Diego, since he worked in the county sheriff's lab, to see if he knew where the car had been taken. With the labyrinth of agencies potentially involved, it was hard to figure out.

"Anything else I can help you with?"

"Actually, there is. I'm curious if anybody ever filed a missing persons report on Buddy Wheeler?"

"Buddy Wheeler? Not sure I'm familiar with him. Was this recent? We found a guy wandering on San Carlos earlier this week…"

"No, this was way before your time. Maybe a year and a half ago? You were probably still in middle school."

Officer Hancock gave me a wry smile. "Yeah, yeah, I look young. I get it." He clicked into the computer on his desk. "Nothing that I see in here on him."

"His name doesn't come up at all?"

"I didn't say that. There are some old complaints against him in the police log. Actually, there are a lot of complaints against him, most for having trees removed when they weren't supposed to be and cutting back neighbors' trees that he claimed marred the view from his house."

If there was one thing Carmelites loved more than their dogs, it was their trees.

Chapter Ten

"It's all public record, so I suppose it's no problem letting you know that the complaint came from Parker near 4th."

"So I'm guessing that's where he lived."

"Why are you asking about him?"

"Just curious. He seems to have left rather abruptly, so I'm interested in learning more about the circumstances."

"If there's anything more I can do to help, just let me know."

"Thanks, I appreciate that, officer."

With that, I continued back down the hill toward town. I noted (and photographed) more new shops and restaurants—heck, I was still doing my job, right?—before ducking into the post office. For those who haven't been to Carmel-by-the-Sea, the post office would probably come as a surprise. With the powers-that-be staying with the colorful names given to their houses in the early 1900s when Carmel was still a village making mail delivery difficult, everyone had a post office box. That meant the post office was filled with hundreds of small copper-colored boxes as far as the eye could see. Down one of the hallways holding the boxes, I found the door where people could ask for packages at times when the front counter was closed (aka nights and weekends). There was a note saying, "ring bell for service," but before I could even ring it, I could tell it was old Mr. Bogino sorting mail in the back. His cacophony of grunts and throat clearing was legendary. He still looked exactly the same as well with his thinning hair, Coke-bottle glasses, and a heavyset frame he still cinched into his postal uniform.

"Hey there, Mr. Bogino," I said. "I see you are still on the job."

"Just occasionally on the weekends to help out," he said, before looking up and realizing who he was talking to. "Sam! I heard you were back in town. How's it going?"

"Good. I'm tooling around town for a story for *Carmel Today*."

"You don't say. How's your dad?"

"Hanging in there. He has good days and bad."

"Don't we all. What brings you in, besides, you know, the mail? Usually, I see Henry in here picking it up."

"I was curious about Buddy Wheeler. Did you know him?"

Mr. Bogino rolled his eyes. "Of course. I know everybody, Sam, and he cut quite the swath through the city."

"Silly question. So, I'm curious. What happened to him?"

He shrugged his shoulders. "No idea. But you're not alone in wondering. Everyone said he moved somewhere, but I can tell you he never put in a forwarding address. We've got boxes of mail back there that no one has ever picked up."

"That's weird, right?"

"Very, but he always was a bit of an odd duck."

"So I hear. And his house was on Parker?"

Chapter Ten

"Yep, second from 4th, west side, perched over that little ravine that runs down the hill to the entrance to Pebble Beach."

"Thanks, Mr. Bogino."

The street he mentioned was a little too far for me to be able to walk over to and then get back home at a reasonable hour. With the sun already starting to set and me still needing to pack for my trip through Monterey, Pacific Grove, and Pebble Beach, I decided to instead swing by and take a look on my way to Monterey the following morning.

CHAPTER ELEVEN

The next morning, I again threw my overnight bag back into my trusty RAV-4, this time to head in the direction of Monterey. When I went into the main house to leave a note for Henry, already off teaching one of his classes at the Monterey School of Law, I saw the *Carmel Today* magazine Mona had brought me still sitting on the coffee table and picked it up to take with me.

Instead of going straight up to Highway 1, I took a circuitous route through town and over to the northwest part of Carmel-by-the-Sea. The streets on this side of town were filled with even more steep hills and canyons than those near our house down by the point. After a few missed turns and small one-way streets, I found Parker Street where it hit 4th, and then a small house that matched the description of the one Mr. Bogino

Chapter Eleven

had given me. The fog had rolled in, and most houses still had their outdoor lights on, but this one was completely dark. The one to its right, perched right above the cliff with a big construction fence and sign on it, was also dark.

I parked my car and walked across the street to the carport belonging to Buddy Wheeler's house. It was flush with the street and what looked to be the top level of the house, which was built into the side of the hill. Layers of dust covered the trash bins lined up on the side of the carport next to the construction site. On the other side, a slatted gate led to a short flight of stairs down to a walkway and the front door of the house, and then continued on around the side of the house to what I'm assuming was a deck.

As I was tiptoeing around checking things out, I felt a buzz from the phone in my pocket. Chelsea's name popped up. Ugh.

"Hi, Chelsea. How are you doing?"

"I'm fine," she said, sounding exasperated that I would even ask. "I wanted to check to make sure you are on your way to Monterey to meet Katie."

"I am, Chelsea, but there's no need to check up on me. I know how to do my job."

"But I'm SO bored. I'm just sitting in this stupid hospital with nothing to do." Did the girl not have any friends? Was that a rhetorical question?

"Then bug Tom or Stacy or Ben or, really, anyone else on the staff. I'm sure there's some type issues they could use your help with."

Saying that, something triggered in my brain, but before I could figure out what it was, Chelsea continued. "I tried," she whined. "They're not picking up at the office yet."

I really wanted to get Chelsea off the phone so offered: "How about your auntie Barb? Maybe she has a project for you."

Silence. That worked. "Okay, fine," Chelsea said. "Say hi to Katie for me."

"I will," I said, and then realized I had a question for her. "Chelsea?"

"Yes?" Still with the exasperated tone.

"Has anyone followed up with you about the accident?"

"You mean besides you?"

"Yes," I said (not including the word "idiot" like I wanted to). "As in law enforcement."

"An investigator came by the hospital the other day to get my statement."

"What kind of investigator?"

"What do you mean?"

"Male, female? Sheriff, CHP, district attorney?"

"Female, but how would I know the rest?"

"Did she introduce herself? Give you her card? Was she wearing a uniform?"

"I don't remember. There were doctors and nurses all around me at the time. Everybody was talking. I just told her what I've told everybody: I don't remember anything until waking up on that cliff."

"And why were you headed south when you left the gallery?"

Chapter Eleven

At that question, Chelsea got angry. "Sam, aren't you supposed to be on your way to Monterey?"

"Hey, you called me!" And, with that, she hung up. *FU Chelsea*, I thought, and then returned to the scene at hand.

I put my phone back in my pocket and continued poking around Buddy Wheeler's house. Suddenly, I felt another vibration—this one furry and down around my shin. I looked down to find a large cat with long fur splotched with white, black, and orange markings—yes, a CAT in CARMEL!—down by my feet.

"Well, hello there, and who might you be?"

The creature, who was larger than Cornwall—heck, it was larger than many of the dogs I'd seen around town—kept circling my legs like it was a linebacker trying to take me down. I bent down to greet him/her/it face-to-face and noticed the markings on its face created an almost yin-and-yang symbol, with orange and black spiraling down each side of its nose.

"Yes?"

"-eow," it answered. I swear it answered me. I mean, I might not know from cats, but I know when a creature is responding to my voice. It was a high-pitched sound that I guess sounded a bit like the "meow" people attributed to cats but really was more of a squeak.

"What are you trying to tell me, little guy?"

"-eow -eow -eow." Or (to me) squeak, squeak squeak.

"Too many dogs in this town? Yes, yes, that is true."

Okay, so I didn't know that's what the cat was saying, but it could be, and it wouldn't be wrong.

"-eow, -eow, -eow."

"But you like the trees? Yes, everybody likes the trees," I said, wondering just how crazy I looked talking to a cat.

"I think she likes you," I heard a voice call in the distance as if in answer to my question. "And as I'm sure you know, calicos are very picky about the people they choose."

I looked down the street. A few houses away, an older woman waved at me.

"Is this your cat?" I asked, walking down the street to get closer. The cat followed right behind me, continuing to try to kill me by twisting this way and that through my legs.

"No. She belongs to that house."

"This house?" I asked, pointing to the house I assumed belonged to Buddy Wheeler.

"Yup."

"I thought that was Buddy Wheeler's house."

"It is."

"I thought he moved away."

"That's the word on the street," the woman said, laughing. "Literally, everyone who lives on this street has discussed it. That and the fact the one next door has been under renovation for more than three years with nary a person ever to be seen. But that's neither here nor there. With

Chapter Eleven

Buddy, one day a little over a year ago he was gone, but the cat was still there."

He didn't take his cat with him? Now that was really strange.

"I was told he and the cat were inseparable."

"They were."

"That's weird, then, right?"

"Very."

"I'm Sam, by the way. I work at *Carmel Today* magazine."

"Nice to meet you, Sam. I'm Elaine. Were you coming to pick up something from his house?"

"No. Or yes. I don't know. I kept hearing about Buddy Wheeler and how he left. I guess I was curious."

"Doing a little Nancy Drew-ing, are you?"

"That's actually a perfect way to put it. I will admit that sometimes my curiosity gets the best of me."

"You know what it does to cats, right?" Elaine said with a grin.

"I do, thanks," I said, laughing. "Speaking of which, who has been taking care of the cat?"

"We all do a little," Elaine said, referring to the houses. "Mostly me and my husband, though. We have a cat ourselves…"

"That's allowed in this town?"

Elaine laughed. "Yeah, we've always been renegades that way. We actually run a rescue group that helps senior and special needs cats find homes, so we often have fosters cycling through here as well—indoor only, of course."

"That's so great."

"It can be very rewarding. It can also be very frustrating. Not because of the cats as much as dealing with, you know, *people*."

"Ha! I very much know and can relate. That's nice of you to take care of Buddy's cat."

"Stella's a funny one. She comes by for food in the morning and again in the evening but won't come near us—I'm actually shocked she's letting you get as close as she is. Then she disappears every day. Not sure where she goes. We were just saying it might be time to trap her and help her find a home. I mean, I'm guessing Buddy really isn't returning…"

"It's weird, right? I heard that he bought a place in Palm Springs, but otherwise, he does seem to have disappeared into thin air, from what I can see. No one's come by the house at all?"

"You're the first I've seen."

"If you find out anything, will you let me know?"

"Same here."

We exchanged information, and I walked back to my car. Stella the Cat stayed glued to my heels the whole way. Having grown up with dogs—big slobbery bulldogs—I wasn't quite sure what to do with her so gave her a little pat on the head.

"There, there."

"-eow."

"You're welcome."

With that, Stella nodded (I swear she nodded), crossed the street and slipped through the gate at Buddy's house. From there, it appeared she

Chapter Eleven

headed down a narrow opening between his house and the house next door to wherever she went every day, according to the neighbor. The whole thing was just getting weirder by the minute.

I headed back up to Highway 1. There, I followed the signs that would take me into downtown Monterey and my first stop at the Monterey Conference Hotel. It was still really foggy, so a bit strange to see high beams in my rearview mirror, especially on a car that was staying dangerously close behind me. I was a little uncomfortable with that, and with the high beams on, I couldn't see who was in the car or even what kind of car it was. As I merged onto Highway 68, the car followed right along. Okay, that wasn't so strange—at this point, you have a choice of either heading toward Monterey or over to Pacific Grove and Pebble Beach, but it was still weird enough that my spidey sense kicked in. I mean, who in the world would be following me?

I did as every young woman is (or should be) taught when they think they might be followed and instead of going straight to the hotel, I exited at Aguajito Road and headed over to the coastal patrol station of the county sheriff's department, which was located in the Monterey County Superior Court complex. I was well acquainted with the place as my dad had started his career there before moving over to the Carmel Police Department, and Lizzy's brother Diego still worked for the sheriff's department, albeit at the crime lab in Salinas.

As I drove to the sheriff's station (and, yes, the car was still behind me, although it had pulled back a bit once I left the freeway, making it almost completely hidden in the fog), it occurred to me that while I was there, I could ask them about Chelsea's accident, since the girl herself was obviously no help. I still had some time before I needed to check in to the hotel and meet with Katie, the Monterey County tourism bureau representative.

As I pulled onto the road that led to the courthouse and the sheriff's office, I noticed the car that was following me continued on past. With the fog, I still couldn't see the make or model, but I could make out a light color — maybe white or a really light silver. Great, the two most popular colors of cars out there.

I parked, walked into the station, and was greeted — again on the other side of a wall of plexiglass — by the polar opposite of the skinny youngster at the Carmel police station. This was an older and very burly sheriff's deputy, who immediately seemed to take me in with mistrust in his eyes even though he didn't look familiar to me at all.

"How can I help you?" Officer Taggert (according to his tag) asked. The "help" was a bit on the brusque side and sounded more like "get the hell out of here."

I decided to skip with any pleasantries and instead said, "I wanted to find out who was

Chapter Eleven

assigned the investigation for a recent car accident in Big Sur."

"Who's asking?"

"Samantha Powers."

"Chief Powers' kid?"

"Chief Powers' adult daughter."

"I remember you."

"You do?"

"Yeah. You were always a bit of a snotty brat. I see that hasn't changed."

I'm sorry, what the? Snotty brat? Who is this guy? What a day I was having. First, I have a cat maul me, then a car follow me, and now I'm being called a snotty brat?

Then, slowly, a grin formed on the old guy's face. "I mean that in only the best possible way, of course."

I smiled back. "Of course," I said.

"What's your interest in the accident?"

"I was the person who rescued the occupant of the car."

"Oh, I suppose that was a good thing."

"You would think."

"Well, an accident in Big Sur wouldn't be us anyway. That would be CHP."

"Wait, you could have told me that when I first walked in."

"I could have," he said with a grin.

"Okay. So, after their initial investigation, who would the CHP then pass the case—or, at least, the car—onto?"

"Depends on what the CHP learns on the scene. If it's DUI-related or in some other way suspicious, they might send it over to the DA's office next door."

I looked at my watch. By now, I only had about 20 minutes to check into the hotel and meet up with the director of marketing, so thought I'd try another tack.

"Is Diego Icaza here? I know he's usually at the lab, but he doesn't happen to be at this office or the courthouse today, does he?"

"Nope. Everybody's who's not on patrol is out in Salinas at a department meeting."

Now I knew why he was surly. With his age and seniority, it was pretty obvious he was not happy being asked to work the division desk during the department meeting.

"Everyone except you," I said, stating the obvious.

He shrugged, but I could tell it rankled a bit. "Whatever. I volunteered to man the fort here."

"That's very good of you."

"Thank you."

"You're welcome." He seemed to start to thaw a teeny little bit, but I didn't have time to make any more headway. "I have somewhere I need to be, so I'll check back later. Thank you, officer. I really appreciate your help."

"Anytime." This time I think he actually meant it. Or I hoped he did.

CHAPTER TWELVE

When I got to the Monterey Conference Hotel, Katie—the marketing gal from the bureau who helped Chelsea put together my lovely itinerary—was already sitting in the lobby. I immediately recognized her because of the Monterey Tourism Bureau binder on her lap. I also instantly recognized why Chelsea identified Katie as her "new best friend." Except for the fact that Katie was a redhead and Chelsea a blonde, they were carbon copies of each other—down to their petite size and the blazer-boot combo that Chelsea liked to call out as part of her personal branding. I waved to Katie, and she got a huge smile on her face and strode over to meet me.

"You must be Sam!" Katie said, shaking my hand. Close up, I could see that she was actually a good ten years older than Chelsea—about my age—and carried a very different vibe. More competent and less sanctimonious would probably be the best way to describe the difference. I also got the feeling we had met somewhere before, but I couldn't quite place where.

"I am indeed," I answered.

"I am, of course, Katie with the tourism bureau," she said, laughing. "Why don't you go ahead and check-in? I doubt the room will be ready, but you can leave your bag and then we can hit the road. Oh, I have such a fun day planned for you and the others."

"Others?"

"I also have a group of golf writers in town," she said as I vaguely recalled that being discussed at the editorial meeting. "We—the bureau—figured we would put together a little FAM for some of the writers already coming to town for the press preview of the Pebble Beach Pro-Am."

Luckily, I was now an old hand at this travel-industry stuff and knew that "FAM" meant familiarization trip, which were programs hotels and tourism bureaus put together for writers, travel agents, meeting planners, and other travel entities to entice them to visit in the hope they will entice others to visit.

"We wooed them with the opportunity to play some of the courses around the county—including those that will be used for the pro-am," said Katie. "Of course, we wanted them to see and experience some of our other attractions for possible mentions in their stories as well."

Chapter Twelve

"Of course," I said, smiling (I hoped). She talked in a rapid staccato that was hard to keep up with, but I did my best.

"We will be meeting up with them at the Aquarium at 11 before hitting some of the other attractions. I know you are from the area and are only looking to hit the more newsy stuff for your story, so don't worry—our little tour won't be too extensive." She looked down at my shoes. I will admit I had gone with my comfortable tennies over anything stylish. "I'm so glad you wore comfortable shoes as we will be walking quite a bit today. I sure wish this fog would lift, though."

I waited a beat to make sure she was done before walking over to the desk to check-in. I was indeed told my room wasn't ready, so I left my bag with the bellman, and Katie and I set off on our whirlwind of Monterey sightseeing. As its name suggested, the hotel was attached to the city's conference center. The center had recently renovated its ballroom and often hosted area events, so we did a quick walk-through, and I snapped a few pictures. Then we headed across the street to Fisherman's Wharf. I hadn't been since I was a kid and was surprised to find it was smaller than I recalled, a little weathered, and filled with an equal measure of gift shops, candy stores, and seafood restaurants vying for customers' attention (that part I remembered). Katie dutifully pointed out the scenic balcony used in the *Big Little Lies* series and a cute little tea shop that I found charming and somewhat out of place amid its crusty (in the best sense of the word) neighbors.

We continued along the waterfront in the direction of Cannery Row. As we walked, it occurred to me where I had seen Katie (and her long red hair) before—at the Big Sur gallery opening. I asked her if that was true.

"Oh, yeah, I thought you looked familiar, too. I was there. I love Zeke's work. I used to cover art when I worked at *Humboldt Weekly*." On my look, she continued, "Yes, I'm one of those former journalists who took a job on the other side of the fence. This marketing gig with the bureau is just temporary, though. I moved here because of my husband's job, and there aren't a lot of newspaper or magazine jobs available in the area right now."

"Is Zeke how you know Chelsea? I think she mentioned knowing him as well."

"No, I first met Chelsea when she called the bureau and asked me to help craft an itinerary for you. But it ends up we both know Brody."

"Brody Montgomery?"

"Yes. Isn't he amazing?"

I guess, if you like guys who like themselves a little too much and, okay, are pretty darn pleasing on the eyes.

"How do you know Brody?"

"He helps us with our promotional materials— photos and videos and things like that."

"Nice."

"Yeah, he's great. He used to do a lot of work for *Carmel Today*, too."

Chapter Twelve

"He did? That's interesting."

"Yeah, his grandfather used to own the magazine—well, step-grandfather, I guess it would be, since it's his mom's husband's father."

Wait, so the father of Brody's stepfather—aka Bob Carpenter's best friend—was the old owner of *Carmel Today*? Talk about your six (or, I suppose, two) degrees of separation. How did their relationship affect the sale of *Carmel Today*? Is that why it happened so fast, and Buddy's financial misdeeds were swept under the rug? And why didn't Barb mention it? So many questions!

Before I could ask any of them, though, we reached the front of the Monterey Bay Aquarium. One of the most popular attractions in Monterey County, the aquarium had the customary line of people standing outside waiting to get in. Katie excused herself and walked up to the ticket window. Soon we were being ushered into the lobby by a young man in a blue "Monterey Bay Aquarium" shirt. There, Katie said we would wait for the golf writers in town on their FAM while she checked in with her office. While Katie click-click-clicked into her phone, I watched the crowds of people walking around outside. When a van stopped and a young guy in a polo-style shirt, khakis, and a cap, opened the door and three similarly dressed guys jumped out, I figured it was them. Here they were: the gaggle of golf writers. And a gaggle they were. All male, one was on the older side (balding and rather portly with pasty white skin), and two younger (one tall, thin, and

Black; the other short with bright red hair and pink skin that he had covered in sunscreen).

Katie introduced us all. "Hi guys, this is Samantha Powers. Sam, this is Paul, Ted, and Pete." I knew I was never going to remember their names so in my brain labeled them as Pasty Paul, Towering Ted, and Petite Pete.

"Nice to meet you all," I said, shaking their hands. "Happy to see we all have monosyllabic names. I'll do my best to remember them."

They laughed (thank god).

"It does help, doesn't it?" said Towering Ted, smiling.

"Are you here writing about the Pebble Beach Pro-Am, too?" Petite Pete asked.

"Not really. I'm a local travel writer and not much of a golfer, but I am writing a story about everything you can do in and around Monterey County before and after the Pebble Beach Pro-Am."

You could almost see a collective groan emanate from them. "I see they have you doing more than just golfing while you're in town?" I offered.

"Yeah, we just played Old D, so Katie here thought we should see the Aquarium and Cannery Row while we're in this part of the county," said Towering Ted.

"Old D?" I asked.

"Old Del Monte. The course over by the Hyatt," said Pete, sounding rather aggravated that I didn't know.

"You mean the Hyatt by the courthouse?" I asked.

"There's a courthouse over there?"

Chapter Twelve

"Superior Court, sheriff's department, and other county offices, yeah."

"I love that you know that."

"I used to cover crime."

"Makes sense, then," said Pete. "Well, just so you know, they call it Old D, even though it's really just Del Monte Golf Course because it was built in 1897 and is considered the oldest continuously operated course west of the Mississippi River."

"Interesting."

"No, it's not," said Towering Ted. "Don't be such a doof, dude."

"I'm not a doof, dude."

The older guy, Pasty Pete to me, rolled his eyes. "I'm assuming we'll get to go to the Sardine Factory," Pete said. "We all know what happened there, right?"

This time I joined the two younger golfers in a shrug.

"It's where Jessica Walters picks up Clint Eastwood in *Play Misty for Me*."

"Play what?"

"Classic film from... Oh, you are all too young and too hopeless," Pete said, sighing.

"Actually, we would have taken you there, Pete," said Katie, rejoining the group, "but it's not open for lunch."

Pete gave us "youngins" an "I told you so" look that was shortened when the young Monterey Bay Aquarium employee who had brought us inside rejoined us.

"Hello, and welcome to the Monterey Bay Aquarium! My name is Zachariah…"

"Ruined our monosyllabic trend," said Ted under his breath to me.

"But you can call me Zach!" he continued.

"And … we're back on track," I said quietly in return.

The others smiled and I realized it wasn't going to be too much of a hardship spending the day with these three. And it wasn't, even if their conversation tended to revolve around—you guessed it—golf.

After our tour of the new exhibit at the aquarium, which was as impressive as I remembered from my childhood field trips (who doesn't love adorable otters!), we made our way through Cannery Row, checking out the shops and hotels and restaurants. We had lunch overlooking the water before walking back into town and ending up at one of the brewpubs in the downtown area.

After trying a few of the brews and a series of "small bites," the golf writers were picked up by another van. While I was staying in Monterey, they were headed to Pebble Beach and already excited about the rounds of golf they'd be playing before the press preview event on Wednesday evening, where I told them I would see them again.

I walked back and got the key to my room from the front desk. After taking the requisite pictures of the room and the view of Fisherman's Wharf from my balcony, I plopped down on the bed and thought about all that had transpired

Chapter Twelve

since I began the day. Starting with the visit to Buddy's house and the discovery of Stella the Cat, to being followed in the fog, to my discussions of Chelsea's accident with both her and the sheriff's deputy, and ending with my tour of the sights of Monterey with a gaggle of golf writers.

I felt like there was a common thread (with the exception of the golf writers) that I was missing, but I wasn't sure what it might be. What I did know was that the morass of law enforcement agencies that might be handling the various strands of that thread—police, sheriff, CHP—were making it difficult to figure out where to start. I realized there was one person who could help me, and even though things were still a little weird between us, decided it was time to contact Diego.

CHAPTER THIRTEEN

The next morning, after posting pictures of the aquarium, Cannery Row, the brewpub, and the hotel, I grabbed a cup of coffee and a muffin in the lobby before checking out. My next stop on the itinerary was the next town over: Pacific Grove. But first I would be heading back over to the courthouse complex to meet Diego. He had responded to my text by saying that he had to testify in a case in superior court at 10:30 a.m., so could meet me in the courtyard outside at 9:30.

After parking in the same spot at the courthouse complex I had the previous day, I walked up the steps and immediately spotted Diego sitting on a bench in the courtyard. Hard to miss the shock of dark brown hair that was always falling in front of his eyes. Even harder to miss his long thin fingers brushing the hair out of his eyes, a

Chapter Thirteen

movement that never ceased to be incredibly sexy to me. I felt a little knot created out of anticipation, nervousness, and—okay—lust forming in my gut.

The hair now out of his eyes, he spotted me and waved. The knot tightened.

"Hey Diego. Thank you for meeting me," I said, giving him the awkward hug of someone you've known your whole life and been briefly intimate with, but not anymore.

"Sam! It's so good to see you," Diego said and seemed to mean it. "I have some news for you about that car accident you were asking about."

"Do tell."

"I thought it sounded familiar and it ends up that Marisol—I mean, Inspector Rodriguez—is handling that case for the district attorney's office. Her office is actually in this complex, so why don't I take you to her? I told her we would be coming."

"Great," I said and meant it. Mostly.

I followed Diego into the third building that made up the courthouse complex. We walked through a series of nondescript offices before coming to one that said "Inspector Marisol Rodriguez" on the door.

"Marisol?" Diego said, peaking in. "This is Sam."

I entered the office and came face-to-face with the new woman in Diego's life. I had to admit Marisol was quite attractive, with long dark hair I noticed she immediately pulled up off her face with her hand the same way Diego did—perhaps that's how they found each other. She was wearing a somewhat baggy brown suit that I'm guessing fell under some "professional but nondescript" edict in the employee handbook as she stood, put her hand out, and gave a substantial handshake.

"Nice to meet you, Sam. I was so glad to get Diego's call as I've been meaning to contact you for more information on the Chelsea Plumrose accident."

"Oh, great. Nice to meet you, too," I said and meant it. "I would be happy to help. I'm surprised the case has already been moved to the district attorney's office."

"There were aspects of the scene that the CHP officer called out on his report that needed further inspection," Marisol said in a clipped very "just the facts" kind of tone.

"And then there was the car itself…" said Diego.

Marisol shot him a look as if he was speaking out of turn. Ouch. "How do you two know each other again?" Marisol asked.

"We grew up together. His sister, Lizzy, and I are best friends," I said, downplaying (of course) our little tryst after my dad's retirement party all those years ago.

"And her dad was the chief of police in Carmel," said Diego.

"You're Chief Powers' daughter?"

Oh my god, how many fucking people were going to ask me that? "I am."

"I have heard many stories about him." And then the usual beat before "I'm sorry."

Chapter Thirteen

"Thank you." I guess she wasn't so bad.

"Okay, well, it sounds like we can help each other out, then, Sam. Why don't you take a seat?"

Diego and I sat in the two chairs on the other side of her desk as she pulled out the report and opened it up. "Let me start by asking if there is anything you wanted to add to the report you gave at the scene?"

"Not really. I was a little curious as to what time the accident happened, though."

"From what we can gather from the information on Ms. Plumrose's phone and the car's navigation system, it happened around 10 o'clock at night."

"Really?" *What the hell was Chelsea doing driving along that stretch that late at night?* I wondered.

"Something odd about that?"

"Well, she left the art gallery reception we were all attending around 8. I was with her when the valet delivered her car to her. Although…"

"Yes?"

"Well, she turned left."

"She turned left?"

"Toward the southern part of Big Sur, instead of north back toward Carmel, where she lives."

"That's interesting."

"That's what I thought. I asked her why when I talked to her yesterday, and she got all snarky—but that's also kind of her base personality level so it was hard to say if it meant anything or not."

I got a small smile out of Marisol before she nodded. "Ms. Plumrose told the office the last thing she remembers is coming out of the art gallery and starting home."

"So, she lied?"

"Or really doesn't remember. She said she woke up in the car as the sun was rising, realized where she was and how precarious the situation was, and froze. She said she stayed that way until she heard your voice."

"That's what she told me, too. Was there anything unusual with the car?"

Marisol thought for a moment before answering: "There were flecks of white paint on the back left bumper."

"We're analyzing them now," said Diego.

Not that was interesting. "So someone could have bumped her? I can tell you that car was as pristine as they come when I saw her leave the gallery."

"Good to know." Marisol jotted some notes in the report.

"And something else: I don't know if this is related at all, but yesterday when I made the drive from Carmel to Monterey, I had a weird feeling someone was following me in a white or other light-colored car. It's probably nothing."

"Probably, but I appreciate you mentioning it," Marisol said, writing more notes in the report.

Just then, the phone on her desk buzzed.

"Inspector Rodriguez," she said, pushing the intercom button.

"Your 10 o'clock is here, Rodriguez," a female voice said. "You know, the parks 'n' recs guy who

Chapter Thirteen

witnessed the scuffle out at the pickleball courts in Pacific Grove last month."

I couldn't help but smile at another mention of this pickleball game I'd never heard of before. And a scuffle! As much as I wanted to learn more, I realized it wasn't my place.

"Thanks, Jane. Tell him I'll be right with him," Marisol said, sighing and smiling a bit herself, before turning back to us. "Is there anything you want to add before I handle the case of the notorious Pacific Grove pickleball scuffle, Sam?"

I laughed. "I think that's it. Thank you for your time."

"Anytime." She gave me another hearty handshake and handed me her card. "If you think of anything you want to add, give me a call."

Diego and I walked back out to the courtyard in silence. "She seems nice," I said when we got outside.

Diego smiled. A really adorable smile. A smitten smile. "She really is. And smart. Like you, Sam," he said.

Really, the man's sweetness knew no bounds. She was going to eat him alive. Or marry him. Either way, I felt for the guy. He didn't stand a chance. In other words, lusty gut knot aside, I was happy for him.

"If there is anything suspicious about Chelsea's case, she'll figure it out," Diego continued.

"Good to hear," I said, before deciding to bring up my other reason for contacting him. "Hey,

I'm curious about another case, although I don't know if it's even a case..."

"What is that?"

"Did you know Buddy Wheeler?"

Diego laughed. "Hard to escape him. He liked to write a lot of editor's letters about the draconian measures he thought the area's law enforcement took. Mostly, he targeted the Carmel police, but he got his licks in on us, too."

"What about?"

"Oh, mainly things we didn't have any control over ... enforcing ordinances regarding his trees, for instance."

Again with the trees. "I heard he got in trouble for removing some himself."

"He did indeed. Why are you so interested in him?"

"I don't know. I guess because I keep hearing stories about the ways things were at the magazine when he was in charge and then the fact that he just disappeared."

"Disappeared?"

"I mean, yes, he wrote a resignation letter that appeared in the magazine, but then he was just, you know, gone. And no one seemed to care."

Diego pondered a bit. "He did leave pretty quickly, I guess. I suppose he had burned so many bridges..." Diego said, looking at me. I got his message about burning bridges—I guess I had done the same when I ran back to Los Angeles after our night together. "Maybe people were just happy not to have to deal with him anymore."

* Chapter Thirteen *

Ouch. I hoped that one wasn't about me. I didn't think it was. The boy was just too nice. "And then, okay, there was something my dad said," I said.

"Your dad?"

"Yeah. When I brought up Buddy's name the other day, my dad had this weird moment of clarity. He said something about the guy's cat. And then I met the cat."

"You met the cat?" Diego laughed.

"I met the cat!"

"But wait, how…"

"I figured out where his house was and went over there on my way out here yesterday morning. The house was dark, but Stella, the cat, was there to greet me."

"You've put quite a bit of work into this."

"I just find it curious—and, before you say it, yes, I know what curiosity did to the cat."

Diego smiled and then pondered a bit more. "You're right that the cat thing is weird. Why wouldn't Wheeler take his cat with him?"

"Right? And here's where it gets weirder: Buddy Wheeler's neighbor, Elaine, said the cat disappears somewhere every day, but then comes back at night to get fed and stays near the house."

"Huh," Diego said, looking at his watch. "I've got to get into court soon, but I guess the next step would be figuring where that cat goes every day."

"Any ideas, Mr. Sheriff's Department Forensic Scientist?"

Diego smiled. "Not at the moment."

"Let me know if you do."

"You know I will, Sam. Hey, it was good seeing you. I'm glad you got to meet Marisol."

"Me, too," I said, and I meant it. Really.

CHAPTER FOURTEEN

I headed back toward downtown Monterey and got onto Lighthouse Avenue, which would take me into Pacific Grove—the town located at the tip of the Monterey Peninsula. Founded in the 1800s, Pacific Grove still boasted a blend of Victorian- and Craftsmen-style architecture, as well as a Monarch butterfly sanctuary and a number of butterfly-themed hotels to go with it. I'd always liked the laid-back small-beach-town vibe the city gave off, which in some ways felt more real to me than Carmel-by-the-Sea with its fairy-tale cottages.

The main drag included a coffeehouse/bookstore (always a high mark of civilization, in my opinion), some great bakeries and restaurants, a variety of shops, and ... and ... it was also the home of my mom's former store—the flower shop where I spent many many hours as a child. Realizing I couldn't put it off any longer, I pulled over when I got to the side street where the shop was located and saw the "Penny's Flowers" sign. After walking up to the door, I took a deep breath before stepping inside, something I hadn't done since before my mom's death. The door made the same sound—a combination between a "schwaaa" that meant the frame could use a little WD-40 and the tinkle of the bell my mom put in when she opened the shop 40 years earlier. It brought both a smile to my face and a little pit to my stomach.

At the sound of the bell, two older women creating bouquets in the back turned in my direction. After a slight pause, I heard shrieks—joyous shrieks, but shrieks nonetheless—and the sound of footsteps mixed with two voices I knew very well.

"SAM! SAM! Oh my god, I can't believe you finally came by!" Gayle, my mom's former partner in the business, said.

"We have missed you so so much," said Melody, Gayle's sister.

Before I knew it, I was enveloped in hugs. Big maternal hugs of the type I hadn't felt since my mother's memorial service and didn't know how much I missed until I was in their midst.

"I've missed you, too," I managed to choke out as I noticed the picture of my mom and me at my high school graduation still hanging above the cash register.

Chapter Fourteen

"Come in, come in," Gayle said. "Melody, put on some tea."

"I can't stay long," I said. "I'm just passing through Pacific Grove today. I'm on an assignment for *Carmel Today* magazine and have an appointment with a sales manager at Asilomar."

They both gave me a look that said that explanation didn't fly. "I know, I know," I continued. "How about I promise to make a date for a longer visit?"

"You promise?" Gayle said.

"Scout's honor."

"You always were a good scout," said Melody.

"That she was."

"I'm glad you remembered." I looked at their warm faces for a moment. "You know, I thought of you both recently when I was out at Esalen."

"You went to Esalen? Melody and I were just there consulting with the garden manager on more pollinator-friendly flower varieties to put at the end of the beds."

"That was a couple of months ago now, Gayle."

"Oh, where does the time go?" Gayle said, brushing a strand of gray hair out of her face.

"Why were you there? Part of the story?" Melody asked.

"No. Well, kind of. I was writing about the Wildflower Lodge and then joined Holly when she delivered products from her farm and others."

"Riverside Farms' Holly?"

"Yes. I just met her last week at an event in Carmel Valley. You know Holly?"

"Of course, we know Holly."

"She brings us the most beautiful lavender for our bouquets."

"And grows some other flowers for us as well."

"Yes, remember the hyacinths?"

"The dahlias were also stunning."

"Quite stunning."

I let their chatter flow over me and felt, for just a moment, a sense of calm.

"You okay, Sam?" Gayle asked.

"I'm good."

She held my face in her hands. "I can't believe how much you look like your mom."

"We miss Penny so much," said Melody.

"Yeah, me too."

"Oh, she was SO proud of you!"

"She was?" I'm not sure why I had such a hard time really feeling that about either of my parents. Of course, now one was dead, and one had no memory, so it wasn't something that was going to change.

"You're all she ever talked about."

I mean, I knew that. I did. But it was still nice to hear.

"How's your dad?"

"Hanging in there."

"Your mom and dad were such a funny couple," said Melody, shaking her head. "But somehow it worked."

"Tell me about them," I said. "I've been gone so long, and now mom's gone and dad's not

Chapter Fourteen

really dad in a lot of ways. I have trouble even remembering them together."

"Well, to begin with, she gave him a life, she did," Gayle said.

"In what way?"

"When they met ... I believe he was still over at the sheriff's department at the time. He came by the store to get a witness statement from her for something that happened out in Carmel Valley."

"It was the Highlands. She was making a delivery and witnessed a burglary at the rental house next door."

"Either way. He came to get her to sign her statement and was such a grouch."

"A real grouch."

"Somehow she saw past that gruff exterior and had him laughing within ten minutes of meeting him."

"It was love."

"Remember we had that cactus?" Melody asked.

"We named it Chet." They both laughed hysterically.

"Somehow they fell in love, and he mellowed out a little."

"Just a little," Melody said, laughing.

"I mean, he was still, you know, HIM."

They both again laughed hysterically, and I wanted to hug them again because, yeah, I knew exactly what they were talking about.

"I do know," I said. "I feel like I've spent my whole life either avoiding or trying to crack that gruff exterior myself."

"I know, sweetie."

"We're sorry. We shouldn't talk about him like that."

"Don't be. That is him," I said. "Or was him. And still is, to a certain extent. In some ways, weird as it may sound, dealing with him is easier now."

"I can see that."

"Speaking of which, this might be an odd question: do you still have the plumeria tree my mom brought back from their honeymoon in Hawaii?"

"It's back in the greenhouse. Would you like a flower?"

"I would love one."

Melody went in the back and came back out with the flower, which she encased in a little vial of water to keep it fresh. I smelled and it immediately brought Hawaii back.

"Thank you," I said. "This means a lot."

"Anytime, honey," Gayle said.

After a lot of promises for another visit, I got back in my car and drove down to the waterfront. I took Sunset Drive past Point Pinos—the tip of the peninsula—and was again reminded just how gorgeous the coastline in this area was, with rocks and pounding surf on one side of the road and wild grasses poking up through the sand dunes on the other. At Lighthouse, I pulled in a block to Asilomar Avenue, where the sign for the historic Asilomar Hotel & Conference Grounds soon greeted me.

I turned in and followed the signs toward the one-way roads that meandered in and around

Chapter Fourteen

the clusters of buildings that made up Asilomar's lodging and conference center units. After parking, I entered the registration area in the very officious-sounding Phoebe Apperson Hearst Social Hall. There I was met by a gal about my age who said her name was Nikki and that she worked for the concessionaire that ran Asilomar. Nikki said she unfortunately didn't have a lot of time to spend with me as they had a group on property for a conference, but that the majority of the updates they had made had been in the hall we were standing in—which was quite beautiful. Nikki quickly handed me a coupon for lunch in the dining hall and a brochure so I could take myself on a self-guided tour of the other historic buildings before taking off. Better than flying around on a golf cart, I supposed.

After a quick lunch, I started my tour back at the recently updated Phoebe Apperson Hearst Social Hall, which I learned was named after William Randolph Hearst's mother. It and 12 other buildings on the property were designed in an Arts & Crafts style by Julia Morgan (who also created the more famous Hearst Castle, farther down the coast) in the late 1800s. Yet another of the intrepid women I was learning about on this trip. And, I was learning, here there were more: Originally a YWCA conference camp hosting a variety of meetings for women, Asilomar was founded by Phoebe Apperson Hearst, Ellen Browning Scripps (a successful publisher), Mrs. Warren Olney, and Mary Sroufe Merrill (who had authored a history of Asilomar and its founding). Not bad, founding Asilomar women. Not bad at all.

Now designated as National Historic Landmarks and part of the State Parks system, Asilomar's original buildings were designed around the natural landscape. This meant leaving trees in place when possible (of course!) and letting views determine the placement of the structures as a way to bring people back in touch with nature and restore balance and harmony.

I liked that. It actually reminded me of how our house out on the point was built and made me wonder if any of my great grandparents were influenced by Asilomar or, heck, maybe even knew Morgan or some of those other intrepid gals. I made a mental note to ask Uncle Henry when I had a chance. The final building on my little walking tour was called the Chapel, which held the main meeting room. There was, as Nikki mentioned, a conference going on inside, so I just took a peek and saw that the entire west wall looked out at the sand dunes and the ocean. Not sure how they were able to concentrate with that view all day.

Looking at the view reminded me I still needed to make my way over to Pebble Beach by late afternoon. Although the first of the hotels that made up the Pebble Beach Resorts could actually be seen from Asilomar State Beach, reaching it by car meant circling up and around and then entering through the 17-Mile Drive guard gate. Entry was free for guests of the hotels or members

Chapter Fourteen

of the golf clubs or other entities (which included an equestrian center and a beach club), but tourists had to pay if they wanted to take the scenic drive without doing anything else.

I checked Chelsea's itinerary, where the description of 17-Mile Drive appeared to be lifted straight from the same pamphlet I was handed by the man at the guard gate: "Follow 17-Mile Drive's red-dotted line to arrive at an enchanting world full of dramatic coastal cliffs, snow-white beaches, mystical forests, and iconic golf courses. Here you can discover one of the most scenic drives in the world as you meet the inspiring Lone Cypress, ponder the giant trees at Crocker Grove, digest the untouched beauty at Fanshell Beach, behold the power of the Restless Sea at Point Joe, stroll the boardwalk above the beach at Spanish Bay, and much, much more." You get the drift—all very dramatic.

After passing through the guard gate, I made a quick pitstop at the first hotel: Inn at Spanish Bay. My goal was to make it there in time for their pre-sunset ritual, where I was told a bagpiper would be serenading the crowd—a nod to golf's origin in Scotland and the "Scottish links" design of the course. A sign in the lobby said the bagpiper would be performing from 5 to 5:45, so I was right on time. Stepping onto the patio, I soon heard the sounds of the bagpiper, who had started out on the first tee of the Links of Spanish Bay and was heading toward the patio where I was standing. As the piper grew closer, I noticed it was a woman and that she was on the young side. Okay, that was kind of cool. I took a few photos of the scene and even added a short video with the music in the background in case our art director, Ben, wanted to use it on the *Carmel Today* website at some point.

After I got what I needed, I walked back out to my car and then continued on. I was scheduled to stay at Villa Sassolino, a small boutique hotel that was the newest of the properties in Pebble Beach (meaning it was 30 years old instead of 100). The hotel was adjacent to the larger Pebble Beach Lodge, which I learned from the history lessons in my packet, was built in 1919 as the Del Monte Lodge at Pebble Beach at the same time they built the Pebble Beach Golf Links, a course that for many people constitutes golf nirvana.

So, yeah, if Carmel Valley was golf mixed in with wine and art and farms, Pebble Beach was GOLF and GOLF and GOLF. Plus, okay, maybe a little tennis and horseback riding and a beach club mixed in. In short, it was country club living come to life—with the gorgeous views of Monterey Bay and the dense Del Monte Forest as a backdrop.

I mean, I get it. The place is golf heaven for a lot of people. Still. Ugh. Here I was moving back into the world of golf.

CHAPTER FIFTEEN

When I arrived at my hotel a little after sunset, I checked in for my two-night stay with a very nice desk clerk. There was no other greeting from the staff until I got to my room. There, I found a welcome card from the complex's general manager and director of sales and marketing, along with a gift bag and a bottle of champagne with two glasses and a plate filled with fancy cheese, crackers, and fruit. Okay, that was nice. The card said they were sorry they weren't there in person to greet me, but that they would see me the following evening at the Pebble Beach Pro-Am preview reception that *Carmel Today* was in-part sponsoring. In the meantime, I was welcome to enjoy dinner at any one of their outlets on them. I should just sign it to the room, and it would be taken care of.

A free night. That was kind of nice. I figured any hotel that let me just wander around probably was pretty secure in what they were offering.

I opened the gift bag, which included a set of golf balls, a Pebble Beach cap, and a similarly logoed vest. Sassy—and/or I guess they knew I didn't have any real golf clothes for the lesson I was scheduled to take the next day. At least for that, I would be joined by Stiletto Stacy, who I was assured was well versed in the ways of the golf world.

As I touched the top of the bottle of champagne, it triggered memories of my last night in Maui and sitting out on the lanai with Roger Kai. I walked out on my balcony overlooking the water and decided to give him a call. The call went straight to voicemail. Darn.

"Hey, Roger. I'm sitting on a balcony overlooking the Pacific Ocean with a complimentary bottle of champagne thinking of you and waving. Wish you were here. I hope you're having a great day. Talk soon."

As I hung up the phone with disappointment, it occurred to me that this was the kind of thing that made me doubt that any kind of long-distance thing was going to be possible. I mean, hey, we'd only just met, and I was a free agent, so maybe I just needed to not put too much energy into it.

I went back into the room and did my usual photographing of the surroundings. I then posted the photos to the website, along with photos I had

Chapter Fifteen

taken at Asilomar and Spanish Bay. That done, I didn't really want to have a sad sit in my hotel room drinking a bottle of champagne and eating a plate of cheese by myself. Instead, I walked over to the main hotel, which overlooked the 18th green (how golf do I sound?) to check things out and take a few more pictures. That was what I was here for anyway, right?

Outside, I found a patio with fire pits surrounded by what appeared to be a mix of romantic couples and groups of men smoking cigars. I walked up the stairs to the lobby, which had a swanky-looking lounge and a restaurant. It was interesting how different this hotel was from, say, the hotel in Big Sur, which as you've probably figured out by now was probably more my scene. But I was here to write about it, not trying to throw any shade.

As I continued walking around, I found a clubby bar off the lobby and heard a familiar voice.

"Well, well, if it isn't *Carmel Today* magazine." I turned and found the gaggle of golf writers I'd met at the aquarium sitting at a leather-lined booth filled with drinks.

"Hey, guys, how's it going?"

They all smiled and held up their drinks as an answer.

"Can't ask for a better day," said Pasty Paul, who was less pasty tonight, with pink cheeks he either got from the sun or the whisky he was drinking.

"Want to join us?" said Towering Ted.

"Sure," I said, sliding in. I mean, why not, right? "So, what course did you play today?"

"Spyglass," said Ted.

"And?"

"Absolutely gorgeous but also one of the toughest courses in the world," said Paul.

"Coast rating of 75.5 and a slope rating of 144," said Petite Pete.

"I have no idea what that means."

"Well, it means…"

"I don't care what it means."

Pasty Paul smiled. "Gotcha. We can say that Pete loved it."

"I take it you won?"

"You don't WIN as much as…"

"You won, asshole. Just say it," said Ted.

"Okay, I won," Pete said, a little inebriated.

"We're buying his drinks tonight," said Paul.

"I can see that."

"Oh, wait," Tall Ted said. They all hushed as a tall middle-aged white man wearing a sweater vest and a Pebble Beach cap walked up to the bar. "That's the course superintendent," he whispered.

"And that is?" I asked, whispering along with them.

"He oversees the team that creates and maintains the courses."

"Sooo, he grows grass?"

I got a collective groan from all three.

"It's not just grass, Sam. It's an art."

"And a science."

Chapter Fifteen

"I mean, you've got to control the height of the fairways, the roughs, and the fringe around the greens."

"Set the cups and roll and cut the putting surface."

"Determine how the bunkers are raked."

I hoped my eye-rolling wasn't noticeable, but they did change topics pretty quickly.

"And what are you doing here?" Ted asked.

"Checking out the hotel for my story. Plus, okay, I have a lesson with Susan Peterson tomorrow morning."

That they were impressed by.

"Oh, she's great," said Ted.

"Man, she SPANKED us when we played the Links. And we were even all using the same tees."

"Maybe she can make you love the game, Sam," said Ted, who was the closest to my age and I have to admit kind of cute, if married (as indicated by the ring on his finger).

"Sorry, dudes. I won't love golf."

"Yeah, yeah, you mentioned that at the aquarium," said Paul.

"More than once," said Pete.

"We get that you're a tennis player, but you can do both, you know," said Ted.

"Not me."

"Suit yourself," said Paul.

Ted smiled and then followed his friends' eyes up to the TVs above the bar, which were depicting—yes—more golf. Someone made a long putt and they all cheered. They really couldn't get enough of it, could they?

All in all, though, similar to our day in Monterey, hanging out with the guys wasn't a bad way to spend an evening. It kind of reminded me of hanging with the Metro team back at the newspaper. I ordered a burger and a beer and listened to their golf stories, most of which went over my head. I had a full day the next day, so it wasn't long before I made my way back over to my room. When I got there, I pulled out my phone and was sorry to see I had missed a call from Roger. Bummer. His message said he was heading out to play some beach volleyball, so I figured I would wait to return his return of my call. The champagne could also wait (or be taken home).

The next morning, I made my way down to the golf course in my new duds. Well, the monogrammed cap and the vest were new. I wore my own workout shirt, pants, and shoes, which weren't really golf shoes as much as my regular ole tennis shoes. I didn't own any golf shoes and figured with what I was doing—taking a lesson—it wouldn't matter anyway. Outside the pro shop, which was located near the first tee of the Pacific Grove Golf Links, I found Stiletto Stacy—who was taking the lesson with me—sitting on a bench. She motioned for me to sit beside her while she finished a phone conversation.

I noted that for the first time she was not actually dressed in stilettos. Instead, she was outfitted

Chapter Fifteen

to perfection in golf shoes, plaid capri pants, and a jaunty pink visor. She even wore a golf glove on her right hand, which was dangling a putter while she finished giving ad page rates on the phone in her left hand and nodding to seemingly every person that walked by. It was some impressive multitasking.

Stacy hung up the phone and took note of my outfit. "Not bad."

"The Pebble Beach folks made sure of that," I said.

"We should get you better shoes."

"I'll be fine."

Just then an older man in golf clothes walked by.

"Hello, Bill."

"Stacy."

And a woman.

"Hello, Sally."

"Stacy."

"Do you know everyone here?" I asked.

"Sam, I live here in the Forest."

"The forest?"

"I know you've been away for a while, but did you forget that's what they call Pebble Beach because of its location in the Del Monte Forest? I live in one of the condos over in Spanish Bay."

"Ah."

"I do also sell advertising in the area. I should know everybody."

"Still, that is a skill I don't have." Yes, it was not lost on me that there were numerous skills I learned I was lacking this week.

"What?"

"Remembering people's names. Or really, the ability to conjure them up on the spot like that."

"Again, I am in sales, Sam."

"I recognize that, but it's still impressive. I tend to remember everything about the person except their name." I briefly pondered and then tossed the idea of telling her about my nicknames for the staff at work and the golfers I'd just met.

"That's not unimpressive, Sam." She paused, looking me over again. "Sometimes you're a little hard on yourself, do you realize that?"

I guess that was sweet.

"I'm glad we have some time to chat before Susan gets here," she continued.

"About?"

"About tonight."

"Yes?"

"This is a biggie."

"Like the winery event."

"Not anything like the winery event. This event is much bigger in scope. That was a cute little local event. This event is a reception for the Pebble Beach Pro-Am sponsors and press and other VIPs. They'll give a sneak peek of the celebrities and professional golfers participating and what courses will be used for this year's event. Things like that. A little perk for the bigwigs. The pro-am is one of the biggest events our area

Chapter Fifteen

hosts every year. It is broadcast all over the world. There will be a lot of movers and shakers."

"That's what the golf dudes were saying."

"Golf dudes?"

"Some golf writers I met who are in town on a press junket the tourism bureau put on around the event."

"See? Not only are people in town from all over, so are other publications. Competitors for the ad dollars associated with this event. Big and small golf magazines, big and small lifestyle publications, big and small newspapers. Now that Bob and Barb and Mona are in charge of the magazine, we're making a new push for some of those advertisers. We can finally make a name for ourselves outside the town limits of Carmel."

"I take it Buddy Wheeler and Hugh Tompkins weren't as cognizant of these kinds of things."

Stacy laughed. "Buddy and Hugh were both useless. Clubby old men who had no idea what it takes to make a magazine like ours work. You have to spend money to make money, Sam. Like us being one of the sponsors of this evening's reception. Thank god Bob and Barb get it. By doing this, and bringing more staffers to attend and you to cover it, we get brand recognition. Then local businesses will be more likely to sign a long-term advertising contract, not just one issue. Buddy just cared that he got a good table in the best restaurants—probably on the magazine's dime—or that Michael MacLean would take a picture with him after he won the pro-am."

"Michael MacLean? Our cover subject? The golf pro at the winery reception?"

"Oh yeah, they were thick as thieves. Buddy would take Michael out every time he was in town and make sure they were pictured together at local charity events."

"Interesting."

"Bottom line, Sam: Buddy and Hugh didn't have the vision that Mona and Bob and Barb have. You joined the magazine at a good time. It's pretty exciting."

"Thanks. Sounds like things were really a mess when Buddy left, though, right?" I asked, and then decided to probe a little further. "I mean, weird how he just disappeared."

"It was a total clusterfuck, excuse my French. But not really unlike him. Buddy had disappeared before. Months at a time. Luckily, Tom picked up a lot of the slack."

"Tom seems really competent."

"Tom is a GODSEND. We are so lucky to have him. He really took care of us."

"How did Tom respond to all the upheaval—Buddy's leaving and Mona's arrival?"

"To be honest, Tom probably would have liked to take over the magazine himself, but he really doesn't have the personality to be the editor-in-chief or publisher. I'm sure you noticed it at the Carmel Valley event. Tom attends those things but pretty much just hangs out with his cronies. Mona knows how to work a room while Tom is

Chapter Fifteen

good at the nuts and bolts of putting out the magazine. I think he's happy in his role."

Before I could ask any more questions, we were interrupted by a tall, athletic woman I'm guessing was about 60 (although similar to Michael McLean, the sun damage made it hard to pinpoint), impeccably dressed in Pebble Beach golf attire. Unlike Stacy's, hers didn't radiate flashiness as much as extreme competence.

"Hey there, I'm Susan Peterson," she said. "You must be Samantha and Stacy."

"That we are," I said as we both stood up.

Susan looked at the two of us. "So, I'm guessing one of you is a beginner and one has been doing this awhile?"

I laughed. "Is it that obvious?"

"Actually, you never know. Dress isn't always an indicator of prowess—but shoes are," she said, pointing at my tennis shoes. "Do you want to borrow some?"

"Is it necessary?"

"If you want to enjoy it at all, yes."

Was that a challenge? "Okay, fine then."

After grabbing some loaner shoes in the pro shop, we walked out to a putting green not far from the pro shop. I was surprised she wasn't taking us to the driving range and asked about that.

"The driving range is the worst place for people to start with golf," Susan said.

That made me laugh as it's all I had ever done, and yes, I hated golf. Did I mention that?

"Might be why I've always hated golf."

"How can you hate golf?" Susan said. "Golf is life." I laughed as that's pretty much exactly what Mr. Tanaka had said about tennis just a few days earlier and what Jen had said about making wine and Tom about publishing a magazine. Made me again wonder what "life" was to me. Was there anything I loved that much, or as a reporter, was I always meant to watch life from a distance?

"With newbies like yourself, I like to start at the hole itself and work our way out," Susan continued when we got to the putting green.

"Got it."

Susan worked on my stance, and we did some putting, moving farther and farther away from the hole. Stacy putted along but also took about a half dozen calls with advertisers while I worked with Susan.

"I'm curious, Susan. What did you mean when you said golf is life?"

"Just that playing a round of golf offers so many glimpses into the human condition. It's kind of the best of life in a microcosm."

"As in?"

"Well, to start, golf is played in some of the most beautiful places in the world," Susan said, pointing to what was admittedly a gorgeous tableau in front of us. "Also, because of the handicap system, players of various levels can enjoy the game together."

I smiled and thought of my game with Lizzy. "Not quite as easy in tennis."

Chapter Fifteen

"Is that what you play?"

"I did."

"It's a good game, too. Have you played the Beach & Tennis Club here at Pebble?"

"A long time ago." Memories of a particularly snotty girl I played in juniors came rushing back to me.

Susan thought for a moment. "One of the things that really sets golf apart is that when you play 18 holes, you spent four to five hours with a person," she said. "You can learn a lot about someone when you see how they play the game. I've met some of my dearest friends and some people I hope to never see again."

"Interesting," I said and then pointed to the larger course in the distance. "Is that the course that will be used for the pro-am?"

"One of them, yes."

"I will admit it's gorgeous."

"Would you like me to show you the rest of the course for your story?"

"I would love that."

We left Stacy still on the phone and walked back to the pro shop, where Susan grabbed a cart, and we were off. While we were tooling around the Pebble Beach Golf Links, I told her a little about the story I was writing and how I kept discovering more about the role of intrepid women in the history of the area—realizing, of course, that I was sitting next to another person who fit the bill.

"We've had some pretty cool women out here in Pebble Beach."

"Do tell."

"For instance, Cypress Point—one of the private clubs here in Pebble—was developed by a woman named Marion Hollins in the 1920s. She also helped create a number of golf tournaments, including the Pebble Beach Championship for Women, and was recently inducted into the World Golf Hall of Fame."

"That's pretty darn cool."

"Darn cool, it is."

"She was also a ranked polo player and swam and played tennis. Really just an outstanding athlete."

"An early version of Lizzy."

"I'm sorry—who?"

"My friend Lizzy Icaza. She's always been good at every sport she picked up."

"I know Lizzy."

"You do?"

"Of course. She's part of the locals-done-good stories they love to feature in the *Carmel Pine Cone*."

I laughed. "Makes sense. I was gone the years she was on the tour, so I missed the coverage."

"I mean, come on, they highlight locals who have appeared on game shows. The WTA Tour warrants at least as much ink, don't you think?"

"Definitely."

"Lizzy has been out here a couple times. She can hit a wicked golf ball, too."

"Like I said, good at every sport."

Chapter Fifteen

At that point, we found ourselves on the southernmost tip of the course, where I noticed just how close this part of Pebble Beach was to the Carmel neighborhood where Buddy Wheeler lived. It was then I swear I saw something move in the tree line in the distance—was that Stella the Cat making her way along the edge of the forest as it reached the ocean? Was that crazy? Even if it was another animal, it made me wonder yet again just where that darn cat went every day now that Buddy was gone.

CHAPTER SIXTEEN

About 15 minutes before 6 p.m., I pulled my auburn curls back into a clip, smoothed my dress, and took a sniff of the plumeria flower I was still carrying around in its little vase for good luck before heading out the door. I walked in the direction of the ballroom where the splashy reception Stacy was so intent on warning me about would be held. It was my third social event in two weeks, which meant it was three more social events than I'd attended in a long time. Part of me was starting to enjoy them a little. I realized that, in a way, the three events—one at a winery, one at a gallery, one at a golf resort—summed up the Monterey area. I kept that thought in my pocket as another potential theme for my story that was supposed to capture the "heart of Monterey" as I walked over to the event space. Before I got to

Chapter Sixteen

the entrance, I felt the unmistakable buzzing of my phone in my pocket.

I pulled out my phone and saw Roger's name so walked over to an alcove just outside the event and took a seat on the bench.

"Hey there," I said, my heart beating just a little faster.

"Hey there, yourself."

"How was volleyball?"

"Fun. What are you up to?"

"About to go to a fancy-schmancy golf industry reception."

"Look at you, loving the links."

"Love is a strong word when it comes to golf."

He laughed. "Gotcha. Well, I don't want to hold you up."

"I have a little time," I said, pausing for just a moment. "It's good to hear your voice."

"Same here," he said, also pausing a beat before filling the space. "Say, what did you end up finding out about the guy who disappeared?"

I filled Roger in on finding Buddy's house and Stella the Cat and how she disappeared down a path into a ravine every day. "How the hell do you follow a cat who disappears through a tiny crevice into a canyon?" I asked.

"I don't know. How close can you get to the cat? Can you attach a GoPro to her collar?"

"That might work. Elaine, the neighbor, said she doesn't let anyone close, but she was totally rubbing against me when I was over there."

"The other option might be from the air…"

I thought of the wine drone Jen had mentioned and we both said at the same time: "What about a drone?"

"Brilliant minds," Roger said, laughing. "Do you know anybody with a drone?"

"Actually, I think I might..." I said, noticing more and more people started to walk past me into the event. "But I better run before I get a demerit for being late."

Roger laughed again. "Talk soon, Sam."

"I look forward to it."

I carried the warm feeling the boy always gave me as I followed the line of people into the ballroom. As I got closer to the entrance, I realized that Stacy was right: This event was as far from the one at the Carmel Valley winery in tone as it could be. The ballroom was actually more of a large pavilion with a sensational view of the oceanfront golf course in the distance. At the entrance, there was a table of very attractive men and women, all decked in black, checking people in and handing them name tags next to a table filled with gift bags I'm guessing we would be handed when we left. I was glad the dress I was wearing was dark gray or people might assume I was one of them. Although, on second thought, that probably wasn't an issue. I was not nearly perky enough. Growling at people when they checked in was probably frowned upon.

Just inside the entrance, I found the general manager and director of sales and marketing standing at attention. I recognized their names

Chapter Sixteen

from the card in my room when I checked in, so I smiled and introduced myself.

"Hi, I'm Samantha Powers from *Carmel Today* magazine. Thank you so much for hosting me, for the gifts in my room, and for the great lesson with Susan Peterson."

The general manager gave a little smile as he continued scanning the crowd. Diana Thomas, the director of sales and marketing, was more gregarious. "You're so welcome, Samantha. I'm glad you could join us. We've been very happy to see the recent changes to *Carmel Today* and appreciate your support of our efforts to promote the event."

Brian Hutchinson, the general manager—who reminded me a bit of Bob Carpenter, but with a bit more panache—followed with (in a monotonous tone that indicated he'd said it a million times before): "The event does so much for the community through its charitable foundation. We appreciate the support."

"Of course. We are all about supporting the community!" I said, in my chipperest voice possible. I was doing my best to be a good little soldier for the magazine, while also looking wildly around to see if Stacy or one of her minions could take over for me.

They both seemed to appreciate my attempt and pointed me to a raft of servers holding glasses of champagne, sparkling water, and wine. I took a glass of the bubbly (wine, not water) and continued on. Once inside, I found a combo playing swing music, twinkly lights all around, and huge pictures illustrating highlights of previous pro-ams. Instead of just one big poster identifying *Carmel Today* as a sponsor like there was at the wine event, there was a series of logos flashing around the room that included the many sponsors of both the tournament and the press launch (ours included).

As with my previous events, I looked around, desperate to find a familiar face. The first one I found was surprising: Brody Montgomery. He had cleaned up a bit from his usual bohemian garb—wearing a black dress shirt and pants with his camera around his neck.

"Well, well, so Mr. National Geographic is also an event photographer?"

Brody turned, looking a bit chagrined to have run into someone he knew. "We all have to make a living."

"Hey, I'm here, too. I get it."

He smiled that quite attractive smile of his and touched my arm, which gave off a little spark. "Thanks, Sam."

"Hey, so maybe this is an odd question, but if I needed to borrow a GoPro or a drone, would you have one?"

"I might. It depends on where you want to use it. Drones are not allowed here in Pebble Beach."

"Interesting, but it's not for here; it's for a neighborhood in Carmel."

Brody leaned in. More sparks. I knew the guy was a player, but I could totally see why. "Either

Chapter Sixteen

way, there are always ways around it. What do you need it for?"

"I want to follow a cat…"

Brody nodded without a hint of surprise. He was about to say something else when Diana, the director of sales and marketing, tapped him on the shoulder and pointed to some people walking through the entrance. Brody pulled a card out of his pocket and handed it to me.

"Just let me know what you need," he said, following Diana toward a group wearing blazers with matching patches on their pockets.

I turned away from the growing crowd and instead walked over to the windows to look out at the admittedly spectacular view. When a server passed, I grabbed another glass of champagne and stepped behind a strategically placed ficus tree.

"Well, hello," a deep voice said. I turned to find Michael MacLean, the pro golfer we were featuring on the cover of the magazine, standing next to me.

"Are you talking to me?" I asked.

"I am indeed." He put out his hand to shake. "Hello. My name is Michael MacLean."

"Samantha Powers."

"I saw you at the winery event. You work with Mona Reynolds."

"I do. Nice to meet you. I'm surprised you recognized me—and that you aren't surrounded by a flock of admirers like you were that night."

"So far, so good, am I right?" He smiled as he peeked around the tree to see if anyone had spotted him yet. Tall, with dark brown hair and piercing blue eyes, he really was quite handsome, if a good 10-20 years older than I was and, as I noted again, someone who had gotten way too much sun for his own good. His hairline was also starting to recede, something covered up in the pictures on the wall by his golf cap, but more evident up close and without the cap. "Of course, I noticed you, Sam. You're hard to miss."

Okay, so that was kind of sweet. I was having quite the night with all the male attention, am I right?

"How do you know Mona?" I asked.

"Strictly business," Michael said. "We met when we did the interview before the winery event."

"But you're from the area, too, right?"

"I am. How did you know that?"

"Well, I know they like to put locals on the cover, especially those who've made a name for themselves outside of the area."

He nodded. "That's true. I did grow up in Monterey. I still have a place here in the Forest and another down in Indian Wells. I am on the road a good 40 weeks a year, so they are really just places to drop my bags now and then."

"I also heard you were a friend of our previous editor-in-chief, Buddy Wheeler."

His eyes clouded a bit. "That's a stretch. He—well, the magazine, which in those days was his personal fiefdom—helped sponsor and promote

Chapter Sixteen

my career when I first went pro. So every year when I came back to town for the pro-am, he would hound me until I met with him, and then insist on a picture together for the magazine."

"Have you heard from him since he retired and left the area? I heard he bought a place down in Palm Springs—that's near Indian Wells, right?"

"It is, but I haven't heard a peep, thankfully," said Michael, stepping just a little closer. "I have to say, though, Buddy is so much less interesting than you are, Samantha. I'm especially intrigued with the fact that you've managed to ask me a ton of questions without revealing anything about yourself beyond the fact you write for *Carmel Today*. Tell me about yourself."

The pheromones that were released in his move closer combined with the compliments were palpable. I wondered if he did this on all of his tour stops—find some youngish thing to hit on. "There's not much to tell," I said. "I grew up in Carmel, was an investigative reporter in Los Angeles, returned home when my dad got sick, and then Mona gave me a job."

"I have a feeling there's a bit more than that to tell."

"Well, now I find myself at swanky parties chatting away with charming golfers. I assume you still golf?" See? I could play the game as well as he could.

He laughed. It was a booming laugh that lit up his face and made him even more handsome. "Yes,

I still play golf. Truth be told, it's pretty much all I do, besides hanging out at events like this one."

"Maybe you can help me with something, then. Everybody I have met this week seems to adore the game. A microcosm of life, I was even told. Do you love it in the same way?"

"Do you know that no one ever asks me that?" He thought for a moment. "I don't know. I suppose there is some love involved. I grew up around the sport. My dad ran the pro shop at the Old Del Monte course, so I started playing when I was very young. I was good at it and winning is fun. As a kid, I liked all the attention it brought me. It's also taken me around the world to beautiful places and I love that. But as with anything, there are parts…" He smiled a rueful smile that was really quite sweet as he looked around the room, but before I could follow up, I heard footsteps and excited voices behind me that I recognized immediately.

"Hey there, Powers, who is this you are interrogating now?"

I turned and saw my three golf writer buddies in what I assumed constituted their formal wear: schlumpy jackets over their polo shirts.

"Gentlemen," said Michael.

"Michael MacLean, good to see you again. I interviewed you a few years ago at Augusta," said Pasty Paul.

"Any thoughts on how the Links course is playing?" Petite Pete asked.

Chapter Sixteen

"Dude, save the questions for the press conference tomorrow," said Tall Ted.

"Yeah, be cool."

"I am, I am. I mean, we played that course today, so I just thought…"

"Don't think, dude. Just don't think."

While they fought amongst themselves, I spotted Mona and Stacy, who had arrived and were standing over in another corner. I gave a small wave to Michael and slowly backed away from the conversation. He gave a rueful smile in return and was soon rescued by an official-looking man in a dark blazer with a different patch, who took him away from the fawning writers and over to meet corporate types I'm assuming were some of the sponsors. An almost imperceptible shield was added to his face as he smiled and chatted with the suits, compared to what I saw when he was talking to and/or hitting on me earlier.

"Samantha, you look perfect," Mona said with a smile.

I felt an insane amount of pride and did a little curtsy. "This is quite the event."

"They know how to throw a party in Pebble Beach," said Stacy, back in her signature stilettos.

"Did you learn anything more on your little investigation, Sam?" Mona asked.

"What investigation?" Stacy asked.

"Sam's been looking into Buddy Wheeler's disappearance."

"Is that why you were asking those questions earlier, Sam?" The usually upbeat Stacy got a bit of a furrowed brow as she asked the question.

"Mona exaggerates. It's not an investigation. I'm just curious."

"Remember, we're looking forward, not backward, okay?" Stacy said.

"Got it," I lied.

Luckily, Stacy's furrowed brow didn't stay furrowed long. She brought out her huge smile when she spotted someone across the room. "Ben, you old dog. I haven't seen you in ages!" she called, before whispering to Mona and me. "He's the owner of Vito's restaurant—I've been trying to get him back as an advertiser for years."

Mona smiled as Stacy walked off. "A godsend, that Stacy is."

"I feel like I hear that about a lot of people these days." Mona gave me a look, so I elaborated: "Stacy called both you and Tom a godsend."

"Glad to hear we have a mutual appreciation society."

Yup, it's all one big happy family, I thought, looking over to see Toupee Tom and Tottering Terry sharing a laugh at the bar. They were again hanging with some old-timers wearing ole timey plaid jackets.

Terry waved me over. I plastered on my best smile and headed their way.

"Sam, Sam, you gotta meet the guys," Terry said.

I nodded in response. "These are the guys I meet every day at Sid's diner near the wharf. We

Chapter Sixteen

nosh and gab about the old days. This is the young dame I was telling you about. She's a sketch."

The old guys gave what I assumed were appreciative grunts.

"Hey, Sam, don't think I've forgotten about that magazine you're looking for," Terry said.

"What magazine?" Tom said.

"You know, the one where Buddy announced his resignation."

"Don't worry about it. Mona gave me her copy," I said.

"And?"

"Like you said, looks like he fell in love with Palm Springs and moved away."

"That Buddy was definitely a character."

"That he was," Tom said. "How was your golf lesson today, Sam?"

"Did you love it? I'll bet you loved it," Terry said.

"I didn't hate it—how about that?"

"Before I forget," Tom said, "the printer's proof for this issue is supposed to arrive tomorrow. Since Chelsea's out, do you have time to come in sometime in the afternoon to give it a proofread?"

"As long as my story for the next issue still isn't due for another week."

"Oh yeah, we have plenty of time on that. Next Friday is fine."

"Then I will see you tomorrow afternoon and will try my best to emulate Chelsea's eagle eye."

Tom laughed. "No need to go that far, but thanks."

"Hey, is that Fred Seulberger?" Terry interjected. "Haven't seen him in eons. Come on, guys."

Tom nodded as they all moved over to see another old-timey guy in an old-timey jacket. As they did, I noticed the arrival of Bob and Barb Carpenter. Barb gave a quick wave and a requisite hair flip as she scanned the room and then made her way over to Mona, Bob in tow.

Soon, the officious-looking man who had been squiring Michael MacLean around the room picked up a microphone and started speaking. The noise level in the room was pretty loud and drowned out most of what he was saying. I could make out that there would be more details about the upcoming tournament at the press conference the following morning, but that they wanted to give their sponsors and VIPs a sneak peek. As the crowd moved forward a bit to hear more, I moved back since I wasn't really writing about the tournament itself. The man with the mic rattled off the names of some professional golfers who had committed to play, to which the crowd responded with a few oohs and aahs. They meant nothing to me, although Michael MacLean did give a little wave from the side of the room when they mentioned his name. The man then rattled off the names of some of the celebrities who make up the "am" (amateur) portion of the pro-am. In addition to prominent local types—both men and women, I was surprised to see, since the professional side was all men—they included athletes and actors I'd never heard of plus some

Chapter Sixteen

comedians I had, including Bill Murray who was a bit of a regular from what I could see from the pictures of previous events.

"He's been a boon to the proceedings these last few decades," Terry whispered, suddenly beside me. "We had a few years there where the pro-am became a little humorless, which was a shame after the likes of Dean Martin and Bob Hope. Now those guys were funny."

"Thanks, Terry."

As the guy wrapped up his remarks, I noticed Barb talking to Stacy in the corner. I don't think I'm the paranoid type, but I didn't like the way Barb kept looking over at me while they were talking. I gave a little nod to her and not long after saw her making a beeline toward me.

"Stacy tells me you keep asking about Buddy and the sale of the magazine," Barb said, grabbing my arm roughly and brusquely pulling me aside.

"Uh, yeah, I've just been a little curious."

"This talk is not helping us, Sam," Barb said with such a vicious hiss that it completely changed the countenance of her face—and not in a good way. "Perhaps you should stop sticking your nose into places where you don't belong and just do your job, which I think for tonight is probably done."

With that, she released my arm and strode off with an aggressive hair flip I no longer envied. I felt my cheeks turn red and my eyes well up in embarrassment while the rest of me kind of froze in a state of shock. I looked around the room to see if anyone noticed what just happened or if I could find Mona. I couldn't see her or even my golf writer buddies. Everyone else was immersed in their own conversations. I stood there, alone in a sea of people, realizing just how much I didn't belong there.

CHAPTER SEVENTEEN

As soon as I could do it without anyone noticing, I snuck out of the event and ran back up to my room with what felt like my tail between my legs. Wow. That smarted. I mean, what the fuck? I don't get scared easily—I did spend ten years on the crime beat at a daily newspaper and have faced down my share of scary characters—but the sheer malevolence that came from Barb's icy tone really shook me. Especially as it happened while I was surrounded by so many people I just didn't relate to: golfers, rich people, rich golfers. In other words, people whose world was so far from mine—not in miles, obviously, but in tone.

I will admit that my first impulse was to run. Pack up my things, jump in my car, head home to Uncle Henry, and never talk to anybody at the magazine or in this town other than my dad, Henry, and Lizzy ever again. There were two things that held me back. One, I'd had a couple glasses of champagne on an empty stomach and the last thing I needed was a cop pulling me over while driving through the dark Del Monte Forest. The other was I thought of my dad and all he must have gone through dealing with people like Barb and Bob in his job as police chief. I mean, it's one thing dealing with low-level criminals, but quite another to deal with the entitled nature of the people that thought they ran the town like the Carpenters. No wonder my mom had been such a breath of fresh air. She didn't let people like that get to her. At all. Now more than ever, I wished I had that quality.

I sat down on the bed, the lovely bed with the incredibly soft duvet, and looked around the well-appointed room. My eyes stopped when they reached the bottle of champagne still sitting in the bucket—a bucket that had been refilled with ice at some point while I was out of the room (nice touch)—and I remembered I had put the cheese plate from the night before in the refrigerator. *What the heck*, I figured. I popped the bubbly, pulled out the cheese-and-crackers-and-fruit, turned on the fireplace, and sat looking out at the ocean in the distance. I mean, if I was going to wallow in self-pity, I was going to do it right.

I kept spiraling back to what I was doing there. I didn't mean Pebble Beach, but back home at all. Okay, I had come home to help take care of Dad

Chapter Seventeen

and Uncle Henry, but this wasn't a permanent thing, right? But there was also really nothing for me back in Los Angeles, either. I had grown tired of dealing with the worst of humanity on the crime beat at the newspaper and being torn up emotionally by a dysfunctional relationship it took moving away to finally end. So, where did that leave me?

After a few more glasses of champagne—really good champagne, by the way, so there was at least that—I tried calling Lizzy. I got her voicemail. Same with Uncle Henry. I was smart enough not to call Roger and invite myself back to Hawaii while I was in this very tipsy, wallowing-in-self-pity state.

Poor Sam. Poor, stupid Sam, I thought. Really. I mean. What. The. Fuck. Here I had fallen into the trap of thinking I was one of them. Feeling oh-so-good about all the male attention I was getting and the glasses of champagne that magically appeared in my hand, and even the golf. GOLF! Ha! And then BOOM, I was put in my place by Barb fucking Carpenter. The thoughts kept circling my brain: *I'm not one of them. I don't belong in Carmel. But I don't belong in Los Angeles either. So, where do I belong?*

That was pretty much the last thought I had before passing out. At one point, in the middle of the night, I thought I heard someone knocking at the door. But who could it be? I didn't remember telling anyone what room I was staying in. It kind of creeped me out, so I tiptoed over to the keyhole.

When I got there and peeked through, I didn't see anyone. With a headache already starting, I made sure the deadbolt was set, tiptoed back, grabbed a couple of ibuprofen, and passed back out.

The next morning as the sun was beginning to rise outside, I woke up to the sound of something ringing. I looked at my cell phone. I had put on the "do not disturb," so it wasn't that, although I could see a ton of text and voicemail messages. Ugh. Then I realized it was the room phone that was ringing, so I picked it up.

"Hello?"

"STOP WALLOWING!" Lizzy shouted into the phone.

"And a good morning to you, too," I managed to croak, as quietly as possible.

"Oh my god, Sam, those messages you left. What the fuck? Please tell me you didn't call Roger when you were like that."

"I didn't."

"Thank god or you would have caused that relationship to screech to a halt before it's even been allowed to begin."

"Like there's much chance of it ever beginning anyway." Okay, so I was still wallowing a bit.

"Stop it. Just stop it."

"Yeah, yeah, I know."

"What happened?"

"Barb Carpenter told me to stop looking into Buddy Wheeler's disappearance."

Long pause.

"And?"

Chapter Seventeen

"And what?"

"That's it?"

"Well, yeah. I mean, she was kind of scary in the way she said it."

Lizzy laughed. "Oh, boo hoo, Barb Carpenter was kind of scary. Where's the intrepid Samantha Powers I know and love?"

"Beaten down with a golf club."

Lizzy started laughing, which made me laugh. "I'm going to say the same thing you told me when I whiffed my overhead on match point at Roland Garros," she said.

"And that is?"

"So the fuck what?"

I laughed again. "Yeah. I know."

"Say it with me, Sam: So the fuck what?"

"So the fuck what?"

"Say it again."

"So the fuck what?"

"Thank you."

"It's just… I don't know. I guess I just started feeling out of my league."

"There is no league that you are out of, Sam."

"But…" and I was about to mention the old boyfriend.

"If you bring up he-who-shall-not-be-named again, I'm going to slap you through the phone line, Sam," said Lizzy. "That's your past. Let's look forward, shall we?"

"You sound like Stiletto Stacy."

"Who?"

"The associate publisher. She's probably the one who told Barb I was looking into Buddy's disappearance."

"So the fuck what?"

"Okay. I get it."

"What's on your schedule today?"

"Just heading home. Oh shoot. I just remembered I told Tom I would go into the office this afternoon to proof the issue going to press."

"That's actually good. You can confront any weirdness you feel about last night right away."

"Please don't make me go."

"Go. And then come over to the Paws Up afterward, okay?"

"Okay."

"Good. Shake off Barb-fucking-Carpenter and the whole Carpenter cabal, okay?"

"She could fire me."

"So, let her. Not that I think she will. People like that are all bark and no bite, Sam—and I say that as someone who sees a lot of barks and bites on a daily basis."

I laughed. "That you do."

"Get out of bed, get dressed, and come on home—and if you want to keep looking into Buddy Wheeler, do it. Just don't hide away from the world again, okay?"

"Okay, fine. I'll see you later."

Lizzy is right, I thought, as I hung up the phone. *I am going to find out what happened to Buddy Wheeler*—and I knew just where to start.

CHAPTER EIGHTEEN

At 9:30 a.m.—a half hour before the time of day when I first met Stella the Cat—I checked out of my room in Pebble Beach and got back on 17-Mile Drive. I drove through the Del Monte Forest and at the fork where the road led either to Highway 1 or downtown Carmel-by-the-Sea, I chose the latter. On the other side of the gate, I was now on San Antonio Avenue. Instead of continuing straight over to Ocean and the center of town, I turned left on 4th Street and headed up into the hilly neighborhood where Buddy Wheeler's house was located. I followed the steep and occasionally very narrow road that ran alongside a small canyon filled with flood control culverts up the hill and then over to his house.

When I got back to Buddy's house on the hill, I parked across the street and looked around. No

Stella (and no, I was not about to yell "Stella!" a la Stanley Kowalski). I got out and walked along the block toward his neighbor Elaine's house to see if maybe Stella was over there since Elaine said she had been feeding her. No luck so far.

Then, as I was walking back to my car, I felt a familiar furry rub on the back of my leg. *Now where the hell did you come from?* But there she was. Again with the yin-and-yang calico markings on her face and still trying to kill me in the most adorable way possible by spiraling in and out of my legs.

"Good morning to you, too," I said to her. "What are you trying to show me, little gal?"

Calling her a little gal was being polite. She had obviously not suffered from a lack of food in the year that her owner was gone. I reached down and gave her a little pat pat pat on the head. She looked up at me like I was an idiot, but then as if knowing I wanted to see her little route, started back toward Buddy Wheeler's house. I followed. Perhaps a bit sensitive to the comment I'd made in my head about her weight, Stella immediately felt the need to show me that she could easily make it into narrow spaces that I could not by slipping down between the bars of a gate that opened onto the deck alongside Buddy's house. She then looked back at me from the other side as if to say, "Hello, idiot, open it."

I assumed the gate was locked but turned the handle and, low and behold, it opened. Huh. Go figure. I then followed Stella along what felt like a

Chapter Eighteen

catwalk (ha!) to the back deck, which had a view of the ravine that led to the road down to Pebble Beach, the Del Monte Forest, and in the distance, the ocean. It was hard not to notice that a chunk of the deck rail was missing from the back of Buddy's deck. Before I could investigate further, Stella slipped through another gate and down some stairs built outside the deck. The gate was unlocked from the deck side, but I checked before I went down, and it was locked on the outside. I found a deck chair to prop it open so I wouldn't get locked out down into the forest.

The stairs led to a little path between some of the houses that it looked like locals had created to do things like (what else) walk their dogs. It was perched above a pretty steep drop off over the ravine. As we know, steep drop-offs make me nervous, so I didn't follow Stella as she skirted her way along the side and then down into the ravine in a space that was impassable for anything bigger than a cat or small dog.

"You got me today, Stella, but I'll be back with enforcements," I said, aware of how ridiculous I sounded and looking around to make sure no one could hear me.

I looked at my watch and realized I was already running late. My next stop was my dad's assisted living facility. I knew I was going to get a bunch of "where's the dog"s from him but really didn't have the time to pick up Buster.

When I got there, Alejandra buzzed me in as usual and walked me over to where my dad was still sitting at his seat in the dining room after finishing breakfast.

"Thank you, Alejandra."

"Of course," Alejandra said. "By the way, he's continuing to do really well. We've even been taking him on longer outings without him getting agitated. Dr. Glenn said that if you wanted to take him home for a short visit, that would be okay."

"Henry told you my birthday was coming up, didn't he?"

Alejandra smiled and nodded. "He did. I know it would mean a lot to your dad to celebrate with you."

"Thanks. We'll try to make that work," I said, sitting down beside my dad and looking to see if the glimmer of recognition was there at all.

"Hey, Dad. How's it going?"

"Where's the dog?"

"Buster couldn't make it this time. Sorry about that."

He nodded. "Too bad."

"But, hey, check this out. I met the cat, Dad."

"The cat?"

"The one you mentioned. Buddy Wheeler's cat."

"Buddy?"

"The former editor of *Carmel Today*."

He squinted his eyes a bit. "The guy."

"Yeah, Dad, the guy."

"He loved that cat."

"Yeah, he did. Remember how you told me Buddy—the guy—was gone? Well, he is, but the cat is still wandering around."

Chapter Eighteen

"That's weird."

"Very weird."

"Odd the way the guy left."

"You mentioned that. I'm following up on it."

He looked at me, and for a brief moment, it was like I could see right back into his brain where the synapses were still synapsing. "Good idea."

"Thanks, Dad."

Then the brain fog returned. "So ... where's the dog?"

"Next time, Dad. Next time."

With that, I headed home to drop off my stuff. I left a note for Uncle Henry on the kitchen counter that said I was sorry for all the crazy messages the night before and that I would explain when I got home. Then I went over to the *Carmel Today* offices to help proofread the final printer's proof of the new issue. I didn't have a lot of time, so instead of walking into town, I took my car and parked a couple blocks away to avoid the two-hour time limit enforced in the downtown core.

I settled into my desk and saw the proof sitting there. While some magazines had gone digital with their printer's proofs, Tom was still an old-school guy and liked getting a hard copy. As I flipped through the pages, I did things like checking the headers (which, as I had been taught at the paper, were sometimes missed by proofreaders looking for tiny things like missed commas) and footers, in addition to headlines and body copy. There was a part of me (the snarkier part of me, I will admit) that kept thinking "what would Chelsea be looking for?" I didn't find any of the picayune typesetting issues she obsessed about like widows or orphans or type touching... *or type touching...*

That's when I realized what had been so weird in that editor's letter from Buddy Wheeler announcing his resignation: There was obvious type touching in the headline. I would have to wait until I got home to pull the magazine out of my bag and make sure, but I was almost positive that where it said "A Fond Farewell to Carmel" the r and the m in Carmel were totally touching. That meant that Buddy didn't write—or at least didn't flow it himself into the InDesign program or proof it at all. I mean, maybe he was just in a hurry at the time. From what Mona and Tom and Stacy—and even Barb and Michael MacLean—had said, the guy was fleeing with some pretty substantial charges about to come out against him. Still...

I kept pondering the implications as I dropped the proof by Tom's desk.

"I found a few small copy things, but really, everything looks good as far as I can see, Tom."

"Thanks, Sam."

"Congrats on getting the issue out."

"Yes, now we get to have that lovely sense of accomplishment before starting up the big issue next week."

"Doing the happy dance of completion then, I guess, huh?"

Chapter Eighteen

"Happy dance of completion indeed." He moved his arms in a motion that looked like one of the characters from *A Charlie Brown Christmas*. Made me laugh.

"I'll make sure to have my story into you next Friday. Have a great weekend, Tom."

"Thanks, Sam."

I made my goodbyes to everyone else in the office and headed in the direction of Lizzy's café. As I walked by the cars on the street, I again noticed just how many of them were white or light gray. *They are the most popular colors,* I reminded myself. I also remembered a little factoid from the communications course I took as an undergrad at UCLA about selective attention and how we filter things based on their relevance to us. I suppose it made sense I was noticing them more after my interaction with the light-colored car a few days earlier. Still, there were a lot—and one in particular that I noted had a little front-end damage.

"What's the matter with you? You look like you've seen a ghost," Lizzy said when I got there.

"I'm not sure if I have or not. Just a lot of weird things are starting to add up, except I don't want them to."

"That's not good."

"No, it isn't."

"Well, have a drink and we'll figure out things from here," Lizzy said, pulling out her cell phone.

CHAPTER NINETEEN

The next morning, I again made my way over to Buddy Wheeler's house. I reached the house and waited and, yep, the minute I turned my back, there was Stella the Cat there to greet (and/or try to kill) me. I again followed Stella back onto the back deck and then watched as she headed down through the gate to the ravine below before calling Lizzy.

"Okay, she's off."

"10-4, good buddy."

"Yeah, right. Just don't screw it up."

Lizzy laughed. I heard her talking to someone in the background and set my phone down on a chair, so I could pick up the binoculars I'd brought from the house. Far down below, I saw a large white piece of plastic whir through the air and start to follow Stella the Cat down the hill. I

Chapter Nineteen

realized I had moved a little too close to the part of the deck where the railing was missing when I heard footsteps behind me.

"I'm not sure what you think you are going to find down there."

I turned and found Tom—toupee and all—standing behind me.

"I think you do," I said, sad to have been right. "I'm also guessing that was your car with the dent in the front bumper that I saw yesterday on the street."

"Smart girl."

Tom took a step toward me. I held my ground but instinctively put my hand behind my back to grab the part of the railing that hadn't broken away. It didn't have the strongest feel to it, but it was all I had at the moment.

"So, what happened?" I asked.

"What do you mean what happened?"

"Where do you want to start? Buddy Wheeler? Chelsea?"

He scoffed. "She's ridiculous."

"I'll give you that, but not sure it's a reason to run her off the road."

"Oh, I didn't run her off the road. Please. That little tap was just supposed to wake her up. What an idiot. She made a snippy remark to me at the gallery about how my days were numbered and her generation would be taking over. I ignored it, of course. Then when I was heading home after my dinner, she was suddenly in front of me—hard to miss that car of hers with that ridiculous red color…"

"Vermillion," I said, even though I knew I probably shouldn't have.

"Yes, blasted vermillion! Plus the vanity license plate, of course. Chelsea was driving like a crazy person. Weaving, slowing to a crawl, and then speeding up. Probably texting. Who knows? I thought I would just give her a little tap before driving around her. I had no idea she went off the side of the road."

I'm not sure how much I believed him but was in no place to argue. However, he was just getting started.

"You don't understand, Sam. I've been at the magazine for 30 years. 30 years! And they bring in that whippersnapper to take my job."

"Chelsea? Chelsea wasn't taking anyone's job."

"Wasn't she? Give her time. She had Barb wrapped around her little finger. It was enough what I went through with Mona. I trained Mona, you know. She interned at the magazine every summer through college. Then she comes back from New York like she's the conquering hero to take over the magazine after Buddy left. It was my turn, Sam. Mine."

"So … what happened to Buddy? I know he didn't write that resignation letter."

Tom sighed. "Damn type touching, eh?"

"You can't unsee it once someone points it out."

"I probably should have put the little spaces in. I don't know. Somehow it felt good not to. No,

Chapter Nineteen

frigging Buddy didn't post the letter. But he was leaving. That part was true. He had to. He was in a lot of financial trouble and had been intimating that he would be taking off. I was ecstatic as it was finally going to be my chance to run the magazine myself. Complete control. I was even putting together an ownership group together to buy the magazine from Hugh.

"Then Buddy called me—summoned me, I should say—to his house, this house, to let me know he was leaving the next day. He handed me a handwritten version of his resignation letter to type into the magazine like I was his lackey. Said he was leaving town sooner than expected as people were starting to figure out he had been skimming money. Hugh was going to quietly sell to Bob and Barb, and this way they'd both keep their so-called reputations intact. It was all about appearances, naturally."

I nodded in what I hoped was a sympathetic manner.

"I begged him to wait and let me buy it myself. I had the investors set. Buddy said no way because he needed the money Hugh had promised him to disappear, and Hugh already had the Carpenters on the hook. He was just going to leave me high and dry. Buddy had already run the magazine almost into the ground. I was the one who kept it going. ME! And now he was being paid to disappear and wasn't even going to let me take it over."

More sympathetic nodding on my part.

"Anyway, we were here talking on the deck, and I was so angry I will admit I felt like slugging him. Just popping him right in the jaw. But I didn't hit him. Really, I didn't. I took a step in his direction. He backed up and, well, the fence gave away—really it did. I don't think he ever took care of anything in his life so I'm guessing the wood was rotted…"

Not a comforting thought as I stood next to that particular wood.

"…and he fell back. I swear, Sam, he just fell. I ran down the hill to try to find him in the forest, but it was dark and had started raining, and I couldn't find him. It had been raining off and on for a few days, and I realized that all that water heading down the hill was being funneled into the culverts. I figured that if he'd gone into one of those, he would end up down at the ocean, but I never found him. I looked for him both in the forest and down by the ocean for three days, but he really did just disappear into thin air."

"You never thought to call anybody?"

"I don't know. I was a little crazed by that point…"

A little? I thought. *What a whackadoodle.*

"Part of me wondered if the whole thing had given me enough time to open the door to buying the magazine after all. But when I went to tell Hugh that I was running the resignation letter, he said that he had already signed the papers with Bob and Barb. All the work I had put in to find investors had been a joke. So, I went ahead and

Chapter Nineteen

published the resignation letter and pretended nothing had ever happened. And nothing ever did happen. Buddy's body never showed up, and as you learned, people were more than happy to have Buddy gone and didn't even question what might have happened to him."

"There doesn't seem to be a lot of love lost for him."

"Zero. What's funny is Buddy thought he was beloved in this town. What an idiot," Tom said with a mirthless laugh. "Bob and Barb aren't bad. They at least let me run the magazine for the first few months. We put out some nice issues. Then they brought Mona in, and well, you know the rest."

I nodded and let a little time go by before saying "So, what now, Tom?"

Tom looked at me and instead of continuing forward to try to push or harm me in any way, sat down in one of the deck chairs, dejected.

"I don't know. I'm not going to hurt you, Sam."

"I know you aren't. Just like you weren't going to hurt me that day you followed me to Monterey."

Tom looked over and gave me a wry smile. And yes, I realized the man's repertoire of smiles ran from mirthless to wry. What a sad commentary, huh?

"Yeah, I swing by here every now and then, and noticed you talking to Elaine…"

It was then that I saw Marisol, aka Inspector Rodriguez, and Diego walking down to the back deck. Marisol had her gun out. I gestured it wasn't necessary as I nodded to Tom sitting dejectedly in the chair.

Then I picked up my phone. "Thanks, Lizzy, for contacting Diego and Marisol."

"Happy to, Sam."

"Did you find ... well, you know?"

"Yeah. I think we did. Jen, Brody, and I followed Stella. She went to sit on the bluff above the spot where the storm drain spills into the ocean down here. We flashed a light into the back of the storm drain, and there's something back there all wrapped up in some seaweed. Pretty gross, I have to say. Both the local police and sheriff's deputies are already here and working on removing the grates so they can get in there."

"Stella still there, too?"

"Yeah, she's still sitting on the bluff watching everybody do their thing. I'm guessing that's where she's been coming every day, as once we got down to this point on the bluff, she kept walking in between our legs trying to kill us. What the hell is the deal with this cat?"

CHAPTER TWENTY

The next few weeks were interesting, to say the least. Tom was booked on a variety of charges and released on bail that, to his credit, Hugh Tompkins paid. At first, there was a bit of a tussle over which local law enforcement agency would take him in. Buddy's "fall" was in Carmel proper, which fell under the purview of the local police department, but his body was found on the border with Pebble Beach, which the sheriff's department oversees. Since Chelsea's "accident" was in an unincorporated area also overseen by the sheriff's department, they seemed to be winning the law enforcement competition. All of it would ultimately end up in the lap of the district attorney anyway, so Tom was booked into the station next to the Monterey County Courthouse (sans toupee, which I'm sure was the ultimate indignity for him) instead of the Carmel jail.

I doubted Tom would end up getting too much time, based on the crimes—both closer to manslaughter or aggravated assault than any kind of premeditated murder—and lack of a record. Perhaps more importantly for him, I wondered if he would be able to stay in this town he loved so much. Maybe he would. Hard to say. Maybe his actions against Buddy would be taken as heroic, and he'd be feted in every restaurant in town or when he hung out with Terry's cronies down at the diner near the wharf every day. Either way, it was clear Tom wasn't coming back to the magazine, and we still had the biggest issue of the year to get out.

I helped out where I could. First by finishing my story, which I turned into Mona. I ended up focusing on, of all things, love. Makes sense, right, that a story about the heart of Monterey should include a little love: love of wine and music and art and dogs and trees and, yes, even golf. I may even have used the dreaded word "artisanal" as it summed up a lot of the loving care I found in places throughout the area, be it in the renovations done to historic hotels, emerging artists highlighted in galleries, or sustainable methods added to wineries and farms. It even included—I have to admit—the golf. Let's face it—the greens on the courses at Pebble Beach are nothing if not lovingly crafted in an artisanal way (as my new golf buddies taught me). You add the love found

Chapter Twenty

in all these offerings together with the spectacular scenery—the unique blend of blue ocean, white waves, black rocks, and green trees I'd never taken in to this extent before—and it creates a pretty special place.

Anyway, you get the idea. I have to admit I was inspired and quite happy with how the story came out, as was Mona. Even Chelsea, who had begun rolling into work with her leg propped up on a cart, had very few of her patented "notes." She even kind of thanked me for my part in saving her life and finding out who it was who sent her off the road in the first place, although she never admitted her left turn and delay in returning to Carmel was due to her trying to break into Esalen in a vain attempt to track down Brody (something we all pieced together later). I'd like to say the incident allowed her to grow as a person but what can I say? Chelsea's gotta Chelsea.

Once I turned in the story, I helped the team get the other stories laid out and proofed. Barb was also brought in to help out with production. Her experience in magazines was invaluable, although I have to admit that the first day I saw her in the office I got a little knot in my stomach. Perhaps sensing this, she made a point of coming over and apologizing for her behavior at the reception.

"Really, Sam, I had no idea," she said as an excuse.

I smiled politely and accepted her apology but will admit I kept myself at an emotional distance from her. I've been around enough manipulative people who could turn on a dime like she had that night to know it could happen again at any moment. Thank you for the life lessons, Mr. Asshole Old Boyfriend.

In the midst of all the craziness of production, Mona mentioned that it might take a while to find someone to take Tom's place as managing editor. FU Chelsea did her best to vie for the position. Luckily, Mona told me in confidence that she wouldn't even consider it. I think she knew there would be a revolt, and she would lose half of her remaining staff.

After the magazine was sent off to the printer, Mona announced a new managing editor: Katie, who was finally going to be able to use her master's degree in journalism for something other than an entry-level marketing position at the tourism bureau. It was a solid choice, and I looked forward to working with her, and even more, watching her butt heads with Chelsea. Chelsea didn't have a chance.

At first, Mona tried offering the job to me. I, of course, turned it down. If there was one thing that Tom had for the job and I didn't, it was passion. I enjoyed researching and writing my stories—yes, even stories about my own backyard—but the thought of managing, well, *people* (especially FU Chelsea) wasn't for me. In a way, Tom was one of the people I met on my tour of the area who showed me what it looked like to be doing something you truly loved. I may not have found it yet,

Chapter Twenty

but I knew what it wasn't. Mona understood my decision and gave me a smile. Not the enigmatic smile of her namesake, but a smile that said she was really happy for me.

Instead, I started adding a few things I did love back into my life. A couple times a month, I joined Mr. Tanaka and Lizzy out in Carmel Valley to work with the kids on the high school tennis team. Afterward, we would all head over to Bowie's cidery to meet up with Jen and Holly to share some laughs and a good game of Jenga.

And then, a few weeks later on my birthday, we finally brought some life back into the old house. Starting with my dad. Uncle Henry and Alejandra brought him over from the assisted living facility and rolled him into the house in his wheelchair. His eyes squinted a little at the sight of the place he had spent his lifetime renovating. Of course, his eyes really brightened at the sight of Buster, the bulldog, who greeted him at the door.

"Buster!" he said.

"Yeah, Dad, Buster's here. Why don't we get you over by the fireplace and then he can join you?"

We rolled my dad's wheelchair over to the fireplace in the big family room and got him settled into the armchair next to it. Buster immediately waddled over and took up his position sitting at his feet (or, really, on his foot). Then, Stella the Cat, instead of hiding away, came sauntering over to see what all the activity was about.

So, yeah, here's where I tell you that I ended up adopting Stella. She had already pretty much adopted me when she kept trying to kill me by walking between my legs. I made it official the day after my encounter with Tom by driving by Buddy's old house and just opening the car door. Without batting an eye, Stella jumped right in. Elaine, the neighbor, was out in front and immediately started cheering and clapping.

"I'm so happy she's found a home," she said.

"Me, too," I said. "Keep up the good work with your other cats."

Elaine smiled and gave me a little salute.

When I got her home, Stella walked right into the house like she owned it. Stella and Buster did a few face and butt sniffs before becoming fast pals. I even found them napping together with Stella's little paw dangling over Buster's back foot. Ridiculously adorable.

Now, I watched as Stella circled Buster and my dad a few times before hopping up onto the arm of the chair and nestling right into my dad's lap. My dad gave a grunt when he found the furry beast on top of him.

"What's this?"

"That's Stella the Cat, Dad."

He got a little glint of recognition. "The guy's cat?"

"The guy's cat indeed."

"Huh." My dad started stroking his back. "Good job, fella. You closed the case."

Chapter Twenty

Before my smile could get any wider at the scene, I heard the doorbell ring. Lizzy came in bearing a platter of food along with Jen, who was carrying a case of wine.

"This isn't the Carpenter's wine—it's the stuff I make for myself," Jen said.

"It's a party now!" Lizzy said, putting the food on the kitchen counter. She then noticed my dad in the corner. "Chief Powers! It's so good to see you!"

Lizzy walked over to give him a hug and he smiled. I'm not sure he recognized her, but he seemed happy with the attention, which was a good thing because coming in right behind Lizzy were Gayle and Melody.

"Oh, how lovely is it to see this old house again!"

"And Chet! How are you, Chet?"

My mom's two best friends immediately enveloped my dad in more hugs. As I smiled at the scene, I greeted more of the guests we'd invited over for the combo birthday and bring-the-house-back-to-life party: Holly, her husband Alphonso, and their son Bowie, even Diego and Marisol.

The last of the invited guests to arrive was Mona, who came bearing the first printed copy of the new issue, which featured Michael MacLean on the cover and my "Road to the Pebble Beach Pro-Am" story inside. She plopped the thick magazine on the kitchen counter.

"Gotta love that plop."

Uncle Henry came over and gave her a kiss on the cheek. "Congratulations, Mona."

"Thank you, Henry."

Their hands brushed in a very tender way. I still hadn't asked what was going on with them, figuring they would let me know in their own time. But it was pretty darn adorable as well.

"Oh, and Sam, now that things are back on track, it might be time for you to travel again. I got a fun invitation in my email today…"

"Oh, do tell!"

"I think it can wait until Monday."

"No fair!"

As my excitement grew at the potential of heading out on a new adventure, I heard the doorbell again. Before I could figure out who it might be, I opened it and there he stood: Roger. We had both been so busy the past few weeks, we hadn't had much time to connect beyond the occasional texts. But there he was, in the flesh. Same straight posture, aviator-style glasses, and tidy black hair I immediately wanted to ruffle.

"Hey there," Roger said, taking off his sunglasses to reveal the warm brown eyes that melted my heart. "So … did I mention my sister works for Hawaiian Airlines?"

"Oh my god, Roger!" I pulled him into a big hug. "It's so good to see you!"

"It's good to be seen."

Lizzy walked up behind me. "I'm so glad you made it!"

I turned to Lizzy. "You knew about this?"

Chapter Twenty

"I did," she said with a wicked smile.

"But how? How did you two connect?"

"I am a detective, Samantha," said Roger. "It wasn't hard to figure out how to reach Lizzy based on everything you've told me about her."

"He wanted to surprise you with a visit, and I told him about the party."

I wasn't sure how I felt about the two of them conspiring behind my back, but all of that was sublimated by the sight of him in front of me. I stood there with a stupid smile on my face until he finally said, "Can I come in?"

"Of course! Sorry! Come in. There are actually quite a few people here for you to meet."

Roger came into the house, looking around at the people, but also out at our view of Carmel River State Beach. "Wow, that's some view," he said.

"Got some smart ancestors," I said, "including these." I pointed to Uncle Henry, who gave a nod that seemed to indicate approval, and then to my dad.

Roger walked straight up to my dad and put out his hand. "It's nice to meet you, Chief Powers. My name is Roger Kai. Detective Roger Kai."

My dad looked him up and down, giving him the same scrutinizing he did to me every time I visited him. "So, you're the guy?" he finally said.

As I died from embarrassment, Roger looked over at me and smiled.

"I'd like to think so."

"Working on a case?"

"Not today, but we just solved a few smash-and-grabs in Lahaina."

"Huh. We had those."

"How did you manage to solve them?"

"Roadblocks on Highway 1."

"Solid method."

"Helps with only one road in and out of town."

"Very similar to Lahaina, actually. Thanks for the help, chief."

My dad beamed. *Well done, detective,* I thought.

As the rest of the group mingled in the family room, I took Roger's hand and pulled him outside and introduced him to the succulent garden my mom created overlooking the Pacific Ocean.

"This is my mom's garden. The one I told you I was waving from when we talked. It's where I feel closest to her, so I thought you should meet her," I said, realizing how weird that sounded. "Don't make fun of me."

"I would never make fun of you, Sam."

I looked at his kind face and those warm brown eyes. "You know, I don't think you would."

With that, Roger took my face in his hands and pulled me in for a kiss. It was one of those kisses that radiates from the top of your head all the way down to your toes. Yowza.

"That was nice," I finally said.

"Very nice. Hopefully, there will be more to come."

"I think we can arrange that."

Chapter Twenty

We sat on the bench in the middle of the garden, holding hands, and looking out at the sea. The beautiful beautiful sea.

"So, this is where you're waving from?"

"This is the place."

"I like it."

I smiled, squeezed his hand, and enjoyed the moment. I took in the sight of the blue ocean hitting the cream-colored sand with a burst of white foam, the wind whistling through the Monterey cypress trees, and the rose-and-green colored succulents my mom had planted to frame it all. Add in the sounds emanating from the house of the most important people in my life and the fact I was sitting on a bench in my mom's beloved garden with a guy who made me feel good about myself instead of the other way around, and I felt a contentment I hadn't felt since my mom died. Instead of the pain I felt in losing her, I was filled with the love and the pride she always had in me.

So, I suppose taking a new look at your old hometown isn't such a bad thing. Sometimes, just sometimes, it allows you to see things in a brand-new light.

THE END

Book Club Questions

1. Travel writer Samantha "Sam" Powers is given an assignment to cover the Monterey area, which is where she grew up. Do you feel there are things you can learn when visiting your hometown as a tourist?

2. Were the Monterey County towns featured — Carmel, Big Sur, Monterey, Pacific Grove, and Pebble Beach — accurately captured? Which would you most want to visit?

3. Describe some of the personal challenges Sam is dealing with in this book at work, home, etc. How can you relate to these issues in your own life?

4. What are some of the insights that Sam gains as she makes her way through the various towns that make up the Monterey

Peninsula? How do you feel about these life lessons?

5. When did you start to think something nefarious might have happened to the previous editor at Carmel Today magazine? What sparked your suspicions?

6. Did you guess the person responsible? Which clues early on gave that person away?

7. Sam envies the passion for their chosen field she finds in a number of the people she meets. Is that something you would like more of? How might that look?

8. How do Sam's relationships with friends and family change as the book progresses? How do these changes affect the story?

9. How do you feel about Sam's burgeoning romance with the Maui detective she met in the previous book? Do you think they have a future together?

10. What do you think was the most important lesson Sam learns by the end of the book? Why?

About the Author

In her 20+ years as a writer and editor, Ann Shepphird has covered everything from travel and sports to gardening and food to design and transportation for a variety of publications.

Now Ann is tackling her favorite topics — mysteries and rom-coms — for 4 Horsemen Publications. The Destination Murder mysteries combine Ann's experiences as a travel journalist with her stint working for a private investigator, while the University Chronicles series of rom-coms are based on Ann's days as a college-level communications instructor.

Ann lives in Santa Monica, California, with her long-time partner, Jeff, and their furry companions Melody and Winnie. When she's not writing, Ann is most likely to be found on a tennis court or in her garden.

Discover More...

annshepphird.com

facebook.com/authorannshepphird

Instagram: @ashepphird

Twitter: @ashepphird

ashepphird@gmail.com

Books...

The War Council

Destination: Maui,
Destination Murder Mysteries Book 1

Destination: Monterey,
Destination Murder Mysteries Book 2

4 Horsemen Publications

Romance

Emily Bunney
All or Nothing
All the Way
All Night Long
All She Needs
Having it All
All at Once
All Together
All for Her

Lynn Chantale
The Baker's Touch
Blind Secrets

Mimi Francis
Private Lives
Second Chances
Run Away Home
The Professor

4HorsemenPublications.com